'Mr Shy put down his feather pen and turned [...] boxes behind him. "We'll leave asi[...] How do you like these?''

He produced a box and [...] most beautiful Spiderman [...] other boys had, but the co[...] longer and silvery, instead o[...] – they were definitely thick[...] usual, with an odd pattern, like lots of lit[...]

"They'll fit you all right," said the old man. "No need to try them on." '

It all starts with a pair of Spiderman runners that Tim has set his heart on having. But, with each pair of shoes that Tim borrows from Mr Shy's 'shoe library', he steps into another exciting and magical adventure . . .

Mr Shy's Shoes

JENNIFER WALSH

Illustrated by Jan Nesbitt

YEARLING BOOKS

MR SHY'S SHOES
A YEARLING BOOK

First published simultaneously in Great Britain and
Australian by Yearling Books.

PRINTING HISTORY
Yearling edition published 1990
Yearling edition reprinted 1990

Text copyright © 1990 by Jennifer Walsh
Illustrations copyright © 1990 by Jan Nesbitt

ISBN UK edition: 0 440 86268X

Australian edition

National Library of Australia
Cataloguing-in-Publication entry

Walsh, Jennifer.
  Mr Shy's shoes

  ISBN 0 947189 67 X

  I. Nesbitt, Jan.   II. Title.

  813.914

Yearling Books are published in Australia by Transworld
Publishers (Australia) Pty. Ltd., 15-23 Helles Avenue,
Moorebank, NSW 2170, and in New Zealand by Transworld
Publishers (N.Z.) Ltd., Cnr. Moselle and Waipareira
Avenues, Henderson, Auckland and in the United Kingdom
by Transworld Publishers (U.K.) Ltd., 61-63 Uxbridge Road,
Ealing, London W5 5SA.

This book is set in 12/13½pt Century Textbook
by Colset Private limited, Singapore.

Made and printed in Great Britain by
The Guernsey Press Co. Ltd.,
Guernsey, Channel Islands

Chapter 1

Miss Barker closed the book and looked at her watch. Knights and magicians vanished, and the thunder of hooves faded into the summer afternoon. Tim dragged himself with difficulty back from the enchanted air of Camelot and gazed around at his classmates, sitting cross-legged on the mat.

'Up straight, class.'

The bell hadn't rung yet. She was going to let some of them out early. Ricky and Ben scuffled stealthily over a pencil at the back, and somewhere girls' whispers could be heard. But the smart ones sprang at the teacher's command, hands clasped in front of them, backs stretched out as straight as could be, leaning so far over their heads almost touched the floor behind.

'Right, Kylie. You can get your bag and go.'

Kylie strutted through the room, that smug look on her face that appeared a hundred times a day: when she got all her sums right, when she came top in spelling, when she got sent down to order Miss Barker's lunch.

'Very good, Angela and Susan. Quietly, please.'

They skipped out. It wasn't fair. She always

picked the girls. Tim straightened his back still further.

'Well, Tim, this is not like you.' She was smiling in his direction. 'Off you go, then.'

Tim leaped up, tripping over Phillip's feet, and shot out of the room. He grabbed his bag and was off down the stairs. Halfway down he stopped, unzipped the money pocket in his shorts, and peered inside. Yes, it was still there. A whole twenty dollar note. More money than he had ever held in his hand before, even counting the twenty dollars Nana had sent him last birthday. Mum had looked after that for him, and handed it over at the toy-shop when he bought the Lego space-ship, so it wasn't the same. But this time, even though he couldn't buy a toy with it, the money was entirely his to look after and spend.

At lunchtime he had shown Phillip the money. Mum had said he mustn't take it out, but it was OK to unzip the pocket and let someone have a peep. Phillip's eyes had nearly popped out of his head.

'Oh, boy,' he said. 'If that was mine . . .'

Phillip had had his Matchbox catalogue with him, as usual, and they had a great time looking through it and deciding what they could spend twenty dollars on. Tim liked the Superkings, especially the fire-engine, but Phillip had his heart set on the 1906 Rolls Royce Silver Ghost.

'Those Superkings are just toys,' he said, rather scornfully. 'But the Models of Yesteryear are Collectors' Items.'

Phillip was a great collector. He had shells, and

6

cricket cards, and several books full of stamps at home.

'I'm getting some Spiderman runners with it,' Tim explained. 'On the way home.' All by myself, he thought.

'Oh, yeah. Spiderman runners are nineteen ninety-five. What are you going to do with the change?'

'Can I buy your Matchbox catalogue?' Tim asked.

'Get one at the shop. They're free.'

'But the shop's run out.'

'Hmmm. OK, I've got two anyway. It's a deal.'

They shook hands.

'I'll take it now,' said Tim. 'You can have the five cents tomorrow.'

'No way.' Phillip had snatched back the catalogue and put it in his pocket, just as the bell rang. 'I might need it this afternoon.'

The rest of the day had dragged on, hot and still, until Miss Barker announced that she would read a story, if anyone cared to be quiet enough to listen. She had her good points, Miss Barker.

Tim got to the bottom of the stairs, taking them two at a time. There were a few mothers in the playground, standing in little groups, talking. Tim nearly bumped into Mrs Palmer.

'Out early, Tim? Your Mum's not here yet.'

'She's not coming,' said Tim. 'I'm going home by myself.'

'How's Steffy's chicken-pox?'

'Oh . . . itchy.'

Kylie was waiting for her mother, and the other

girls were playing on the swings, so Tim was the first to leave the playground. The lollipop lady was at the crossing, thank goodness – Mum had said if she wasn't there he was to wait and cross with an adult. The lady held up her sign and he walked across proudly, stopping three cars. Then he turned and set off down the hill, past the first shops.

Normally Tim would have lingered outside the newspaper shop to look at the Matchbox cars, the bookshop to check out the pop-up books, the milk-bar to read the advertisements and see if there were any new competitions involving ice-cream sticks or lolly wrappers. But today he had a purpose, and he headed straight for the shoe shop.

'This is the last straw,' Mum had said that morning when he showed her the hole in the sole of his runner. 'What am I going to do about that?'

'You said I could have Spiderman runners next time,' he reminded her.

'Yes, but I can't take you shopping, can I, with Steffy covered in spots? Where are your sandals?'

'I lost them, remember?'

'Oh, God.'

'They were too small anyway, Mum. Why can't I buy the runners myself? I walk right past the shop.'

'Oh, well . . . I don't know.'

It took a bit of persuading, but finally she zipped the money into his pocket and, with a million instructions, sent him off to school.

It was a simple task, anyway. Tim knew his size – size three – and anyway, he could always ask to have his foot measured. The Spiderman runners were right there, on display in the middle of the window. They must have sold hundreds of pairs already – nearly everyone in the school had them by now.

Tim stepped into the shop, unzipping his pocket and fingering the crisp twenty-dollar note as he went. The bald man who usually sat drinking coffee at the back of the shop approached him.

'Yes, young man. What can we do for you?'

'A pair of Spiderman runners, please. Size three.'

'Size three, is it? Hmmmm.'

The man started to rummage round among the piles of shoe boxes.

'We've got these in size three.'

Out came a pair of plain blue denim runners.

'These do you?'

'No. No thank you,' stammered Tim. 'I really want Spiderman ones.'

'Well. I can give you a size five.'

The man found a box with the Spiderman picture on it and produced an enormous shoe. 'May as well try it on, eh?'

'All right.'

Tim picked furiously at the double knot on his old runner. Why did Mum insist on double knots? She usually helped him when they were really tight. At last he got his shoe off and slipped the other one on. His foot swam in it.

'Hmmm. Bit big,' admitted the man. 'Might grow into it, eh?'

'I don't think so,' said Tim doubtfully.

'Well, then, I can't help you. Sorry.' The man didn't really sound sorry. 'We're getting some more stock in next week. Come back . . . oh, after Wednesday.'

'All right. Thank you.'

Dismally Tim retied his shoelace, forgetting to pull it tight. He picked up his bag and trudged out of the shop. What now? Another whole week without Spiderman runners stretched out before him – and by then Steffy would be back at school, Mum would be picking them both up in the afternoons as she normally did. She would carry the money, talk to the man, make the decisions. Tim had pictured himself arriving at school in the new runners, telling his friends how he'd gone down the street and bought them. You got stickers with Spiderman runners. He was going to produce them for News and mention, just in passing, how he'd bought the shoes himself. Next Wednesday might as well be next year.

Tim dragged his feet as he walked on. He could feel the footpath through the hole in his right shoe. All these people must have noticed that he was walking home by himself, just like most of the other boys in his class. It wouldn't do to cry, with them all looking at him. He slowed down a bit more to glance in the window of the antique shop – the junk shop, Mum called it. Sometimes they had interesting things – puppets, strange clothes, occasionally some old-fashioned toy cars that he could tell Phillip about.

Funny – he'd never noticed the shop next to the antique shop before. It was very narrow, with a door set back from the street, rather shadowy, and a little window no bigger than you'd see on a house. The odd thing was, it looked like a shoe shop. The lighting was dim, but the window appeared to be full of cardboard shoe-boxes, with a single pair of rather splendid-looking boots on display in the centre; and inside he thought he could make out more shoe-boxes, rows and rows of them.

Tim hovered around the doorway. If it really was a shoe shop he ought to go in and ask. It had a sort of funny, old-fashioned look about it, but you never knew. The ads for Spiderman runners did say 'On Sale Everywhere'. In a way he very much wanted to go into the shop. There was something that seemed to draw him to it, like a little voice whispering in his ear, urging him inside. But at the same time there was something scary about the place, probably just because it was old, and narrow, and dim.

The door creaked gently as Tim stepped inside. The shop seemed deserted, but it was hard to tell. The narrow floor space was made even smaller by a counter of dark timber, polished to a soft glow, which took up most of the floor space as it stretched off towards the back of the long room. Indeed, you couldn't exactly see how far back it went, the back of the shop was so dark. It seemed to stretch on forever. The wall behind the counter, as Tim had seen from the outside, was lined from floor to ceiling with white cardboard shoe-boxes; but instead of familiar-looking bright labels, they were marked by scrawls of running writing, all curls and flourishes, which Tim could not read.

A little silver bell stood on the counter, and Tim picked it up. It gave a soft ting-a-ling, and before the sound had died away a movement could be seen in the gloomy depths of the shop, and the strangest-looking person Tim had ever seen emerged and glided towards him.

He was clearly an old man – the balding head and fringe of shoulder-length white hair made that a certainty – but he was tiny, no taller than Tim himself, and his skin was as pink and soft as a baby's. He wore a narrow sort of coat, nipped in at the waist and coming down below his knees at the back, which looked as though it had once been black, but which was now a greenish colour, with shiny patches. This was coupled with striped greyish trousers, and, at his throat, a silky reddish scarf. But the most noticeable thing about the old man was the two pairs of glasses which he wore, one pair in more or less the usual position, the other perched on the tip of his very long nose. Both had such thick lenses you could only see a blur through them.

The old man peered through the upper pair of glasses at Tim.

'You're a new face,' he wheezed. 'Do you want to join, then?'

'I . . . I don't know.'

'Don't know? Don't know?' The wheeze turned into a sort of silent laugh that threatened to suffocate its owner, since he seemed unable to draw a breath as long as his mirth lasted. 'What do you know, then?'

'Well . . .' Tim tried to think of something. 'I

know I want some Spiderman runners.'

'Spiderman, is it? All this television.' The old man wheezed again, to Tim's alarm. 'But if that's what you're after, I suppose you do want to join.' He started to fumble around under the counter.

'Do you really have Spiderman runners?' Tim could hardly believe his luck. 'Have you got size three?'

'All in good time, boy.' The old man put some papers on the counter, a little bottle of ink, and a most extraordinary pen, which seemed to be made out of a feather.

'Name?'

Tim blushed. 'Theodore Ivan Morrison.'

'I suppose they call you Tim, eh?'

'Yes.'

'That'll do, then.'

Tim could now see the purpose of the lower pair of glasses as the old man peered through them at the paper. The word Tim, in the most beautiful curly writing, flowed from the tip of the feather pen. The old man looked up.

'You'd better know my name: Mr Shy.'

Tim jumped. He had been a bit tongue-tied in this strange presence, but he thought he'd been acting reasonably grown-up and confident.

'Sorry,' he said. 'What is your name, please?'

'Didn't I just tell you? It's Mr Shy. Now – hobbies?'

'Hobbies?'

'You're a bit hard of hearing boy. Hobbies. Things you do so you can tell your friends about them.'

13

'Oh. Like . . . collecting things?'

'Yes, yes. Butterfly nets, precious stones – shrunken heads, eh? But also, I mean things like hot-air ballooning, mountain-climbing. You know – deep-sea diving.'

'I . . . I've never done any of those,' stammered Tim. 'But I've been on the Great Barrier Reef in a glass-bottomed boat.'

'We're not talking about what you've done,' snapped Mr Shy. 'We're talking about what you'd like to do. That's why you're joining, isn't it?'

'Excuse me.' Tim thought he'd better be bold. 'What exactly am I joining?'

'The library, of course.'

'Library?' Tim looked around the shop. 'I thought you had shoes.'

'Of course we have shoes. It's a shoe library, isn't it? You tell me what you want to do, and I'll find you a pair of shoes to do it in.'

Tim tried hard to fit this into the things he already knew about libraries and shoes. Finally he said, 'I always thought libraries were for . . . stories.'

'So they are, boy.' The old man wheezed terribly. 'You'll find plenty of stories here.'

'But I . . . What I wanted was some Spiderman runners. I've got the twenty dollars.' Tim pulled the note out of his pocket.

'Yes, yes, we're getting carried away.' Mr Shy put down his feather pen and turned to the stack of boxes behind him. 'We'll leave aside the paperwork. Here. How do you like these?'

He produced a box and swept the lid off it. Inside were the most beautiful Spiderman runners. They were like what the other boys had, but the colours seemed brighter, the laces longer and silvery, instead of plain white, and as for the soles – they were definitely thicker and tougher than usual, with an odd pattern, like lots of little circles.

'They'll fit you all right,' said the old man. 'No need to try them on.'

He put the lid back on the box and tied it up with string.

'They're . . . um . . . Are they nineteen ninety-five?'

Tim held out the twenty-dollar note. Mr Shy waved it away.

'You don't need that. We don't sell shoes here.

15

It's a library, right? Use them, and bring them back next time you come past and find me here.'

'Um . . . Could I have them until next Wednesday?'

'Maybe. Possibly. If you don't find me here before then.'

Tim thought this sounded rather a vague arrangement, but Mr Shy seemed happy about it. Tim also had a strong feeling that he should leave the shoes on the counter and go, but the runners were so beautiful, and Mr Shy seemed so certain that it was a normal thing for Tim to borrow them. He picked up the box, and went to the door.

'Goodbye, then . . .' Tim turned back towards the shop, but Mr Shy had already gone, into the shadows at the back. The door creaked again as Tim went out into the bright sunshine.

Chapter 2

Tim started home at a run, which slowed down as he climbed the hill to a fast walk, with little excited skips now and then. He could hardly wait to get home and ring up Phillip. He could hardly wait to get to school tomorrow and show all the other kids. He could hardly wait to see Steffy's face. He could hardly wait to tell . . . Here he slowed down a little. What was going to happen when he told Mum?

The trouble was, she made so many rules about everything. For her to agree to let him buy the shoes in the first place, he'd had to promise to go straight to the shop, to buy exactly those runners and no others, to keep the money zipped in his pocket, to come straight home afterwards – the list went on and on. Going into another shop and meeting Mr Shy didn't seem to belong anywhere on that list. Tim wasn't sure that his mother would like Mr Shy or his shop, or library, whatever it was. Some of those shoe-boxes had looked very dusty. Maybe she would make him take the shoes straight back. Maybe she would say he wasn't old enough to go shopping after all. He couldn't pretend he'd bought the shoes – it would be telling lies, and there was still the twenty-dollar note to explain. He still wanted to go back next Wednesday

17

and buy some runners that would be his own, not just borrowed.

All these thoughts spun round inside Tim's head, making him feel quite giddy. He was walking very slowly now. Eventually he stopped altogether and put the shoe-box in his school bag, under his lunchbox. That would just keep it safely out of the way until he had decided what to do.

Mum was in the kitchen when Tim came in through the back door.

'There you are at last!' she exclaimed, kissing him. 'Did you go to the shoe shop?'

'They didn't have my size, Mum!' The remembrance of that disappointment made Tim's lip tremble again. 'The man tried to sell me a size five.'

'Never mind, darling. Perhaps they'll get some more in.'

'Yes – he said to come back after Wednesday.' Tim took out the money and handed it over. 'Can I go by myself again?'

'Oh – we'll see. Steffy should be back at school by then.'

She took a plate with some cake on it and a glass of apple juice, and put them on the table. 'Look, I've got your afternoon tea ready.'

Tim had been planning to make himself a honey sandwich, and to remember to wash the knife this time, but you couldn't say no to cake. He sat down and started to eat. His mother went out of the room and came back with a pair of sandals.

'I saw Mary today, and she gave me these sandals that Scott's grown out of.'

They were a new-looking pair of Star Wars sandals – not red, unfortunately.

'I don't normally like you to wear shoes that someone else has had,' his mother went on, 'but he hardly wore them. Didn't like the colour, or something.'

Tim tried the sandals on. They looked all right.

'What's wrong with wearing shoes that someone else has had?' he asked.

'Oh . . . they're bad for your feet.'

'Oh.'

Tim thought guiltily of the shoe library. Maybe Mum *wouldn't* like it. But Mr Shy hadn't seemed to worry about feet.

'Mum,' he ventured. 'Are there shoe libraries?'

'Whatever do you mean?'

'Where you can borrow shoes?'

His mother laughed. 'You do get some funny ideas, Tim. I wish you'd use your imagination when you have to write those stories for school.'

'I did a good one today,' said Tim defensively. 'It was about a boy who goes out in a glass-bottomed boat, and the glass breaks.'

'You did that last week, surely?'

'No,' said Tim. 'Last week the boy fell out of the boat.'

'Well I'm sure it was very nice,' said his mother briskly. 'Now, do you want to come upstairs with me? We'd better wake Steffy and give her some medicine.'

Tim trailed up the stairs behind his mother. He was now convinced that the Spiderman runners had better stay put in the bottom of his school bag until tomorrow, when he could take them back to Mr Shy. He thought of the bright colours and the superthick soles. He thought of the silvery laces, and he sighed.

Steffy was awake, lying quietly in her bed. She looked hot and damp, and there was a new crop of spots, on her face this time. Each spot had a little drop of brownish liquid at its centre. They looked sticky. One, on her chin, was redder than the rest, and sore-looking.

'Steffy, you mustn't scratch them,' wailed Mum. 'You'll get pock-marks.'

Steffy sat up and reached for her medicine. It was her favourite, a red syrup. Tim liked it too, and watched a little enviously as she drank it down.

'I've got some more chicken-pox, Tim,' she announced.

'I know. How many is that now?'

'Twenty-twelve,' said Steffy proudly.

'You mean thirty-two,' Tim corrected her.

'No I don't.'

'Yes you do.'

'No I don't.

'Children! Enough argument!' There was a dangerous note in their mother's voice. 'Steffy, would you like a drink? Something to eat?'

'Just lemonade, please.' Steffy lolled back on her pillows like a little queen.

'You've finished all the lemonade.'

'That's not fair!' started Tim, but seeing his mother's look he decided not to pursue the matter.

'Tim, would you be an angel and read Steffy a story while I get her a drink of apple juice?'

Tim stifled a groan. It was great being allowed to walk to school by himself while Steffy was sick but, like his mother, he was starting to wish she'd hurry up and get better.

Towards the end of *Morris's Disappearing Bag*, with Steffy already leafing through her books looking for the next request, the phone rang. Mum called up the stairs, 'It's Jonathon's mother. Would you like to come and play?'

Tim was quick to accept the invitation. Jonathon was a bit on the boring side, but he had a Lego train set. The other good thing was that he only lived a few streets away, and Tim was allowed to walk round there by himself. Steffy set up a wail at the thought of being left behind, but the promise of some pastry to help roll out soon calmed her down. Their mother came upstairs to help Steffy find her frilly apron in the dress-ups box, and Tim set off.

His school bag was still in the kitchen, lying by the back door. He could hear the others talking quietly upstairs. On an impulse, he reached in the bag and grabbed the shoe-box. There was a porch outside with a bench seat, and it took barely a moment for Tim to change his shoes and put the Star Wars sandals, in the shoe-box, out of sight under the seat. Then he raced down the side path and out into the street.

Mr Shy was right – the shoes fitted perfectly, and they looked wonderful, with the laces glistening in the sunlight. The soles were springy but light, and Tim danced and skipped as he hurried along.

It was a very satisfying visit. Jonathon's mother welcomed Tim warmly, and gave him some lemonade and three chocolate biscuits. Jonathon admired the Spiderman runners, and showed Tim his new Superman outfit. Together they built a new station for the Lego trains, and it seemed to Tim he had barely arrived when Jonathon's mother put her head around the door of his room and said: 'That was your mother on the phone, Tim. It's time for you to go.'

Regretfully Tim dragged himself away. Jonathon's mother gave him another chocolate biscuit, for the road, and waved goodbye. 'Go straight home, won't you?' she said. 'You know how your mother worries.'

'I know,' sighed Tim.

As he rounded the first corner Tim heard the sound of sirens. They sounded very close – and then he could see the flashing red lights reflected on the houses, and three – three! – fire engines raced past the corner he was approaching. Tim ran to the corner. The fire engines had stopped just down the street, and now he could see smoke billowing up and flames darting out of the windows, high up, of a big brick building. It was some sort of warehouse, or factory – Tim had passed it often enough, and not taken much notice.

Tim tried to get closer. There were police cars as well as the fire engines, and the street was partly blocked off. A crowd had gathered, and the police were hard at work making sure no-one got anywhere near the building. You couldn't see much, especially up close, with the large backs of all the

22

spectators in the way, jostling each other as they crowded forward.

A few doors past the building was a narrow lane. Tim had played in this street, and he knew that the lane turned and went along the back of the burning building. Unnoticed, he slipped away from the crowd and quietly entered the lane. He was able to go right up to the back wall, but it was a bit disappointing. There was some smoke, but most of the fire seemed to be round the front. Faintly he could hear the firemen shouting inside the building, and crashing noises. Maybe they were breaking down doors with their axes, or maybe parts of the interior were collapsing. There was a roaring noise, too, which seemed to be getting louder. Tim's cousin, who had seen a bushfire, had told him that you don't see any flames – just darkness, and the deafening roar of the blaze. Tim decided to leave.

Just then another noise seemed to rise over the commotion. A thin, weak noise, but Tim's ears picked it up. He stood back from the building and peered up through the haze. Now he could see, high up on the edge of the roof, gazing down at him, a tiny kitten. It meowed again, piteously, and disappeared; but a minute later it was back, running up and down on the parapet. Tim fancied that behind it the smoke was thicker than before, pouring upwards.

Tim ran as fast as he could back to the street. The crowd was thicker, and he could not fight his way through. But off to the side he saw a fireman go over to one of the trucks and start undoing another hose. Tim ran to him.

'Mister!' he cried breathlessly. 'There's a kitten up there!'

'Not now, sonny.' The man was busy with his hose.

'But there's a kitten, up there on the roof. It'll get burnt up!'

The fireman looked at him sternly. 'There are people inside, too. We've got to get them out first. We're doing the best we can.'

He set off at a run, paying out the hose behind him as he went. Another fireman almost knocked Tim over as he sprang on to the truck. 'Get back, son,' he shouted. 'We've got work to do here.'

Tim went back up the lane. The smoke was thicker now – it made him cough. The kitten was still there, meowing plaintively. Tim felt he couldn't leave it. He called softly, 'Puss, puss. Jump into my arms!'

He held up his arms, but the kitten only stared. It was much too high, anyway. Tim scrabbled about in the lane, looking for a rope, an old ladder, anything . . . but of course there was nothing. He wished he were Spiderman, and could climb up the wall. He touched it with one hand. That was strange, it had a sticky feel – he had to pull to get his hand off. He tried touching it with his foot – and the sole of his Spiderman runner clamped firmly on to the wall.

With growing excitement Tim reached upwards with both hands, clamped his other foot to the wall, and there he was, climbing upwards as fast as he could go. It was like when you get down on your hands and feet and run around like a four-footed

animal, except that Tim was running straight up the wall.

He got to the top and scrambled on to the parapet. The kitten sat with its head on one side, looking at him.

'Here, puss, puss,' murmured Tim, holding out a hand. The kitten danced away. Tim saw now that dense black smoke from the fire at the front of the building was rolling towards them, and he could see flames shooting up towards the sky. There were rumbling sounds from inside, as though parts of the building were collapsing, and not far from where he sat the roof was starting to cave in. The kitten scampered about near this perilous spot, lifting its paws high at every step. Tim guessed that the iron roof was getting rather hot.

'Come here, puss,' he tried again. The kitten sniffed his outstretched finger and bounded away. He looked round for something to attract its attention.

Just then Tim noticed that one of his shoelaces had come undone. The shoelace was longer than he remembered, and shimmered in the reddish light. He picked up an end of it and dangled it in front of him. The kitten crept along the parapet, stalking it.

'Gosh, kitten,' sighed Tim. 'We're both about to be fried alive and you want to play!'

The kitten pounced on the shoelace, and at the same moment Tim grabbed the kitten with both hands. The shoelace was pulled right out of the shoe, and the struggling kitten was immediately tangled up in it. The shoelace seemed to grow longer every second, and Tim had an idea. He wound the shoelace, which was very sticky by now, several times around the kitten, then around his own waist. The result was one kitten snugly wrapped in a sticky cocoon, safely attached to Tim. With both hands free for climbing, he took only a minute to scramble back down the wall. The instant he was safely down, the shoelace dropped to the ground, and Tim had to grab at the kitten. He picked up his shoelace – it was back to its normal size – and stuffed it in his pocket. Then he walked back round to the front of the building.

The fireman he had spoken to earlier was on the back of another fire engine. Smoke swirled around, but the fire was not roaring as fiercely as before.

'It's all right mister,' called Tim. 'I've got him.'

'What's that?' shouted back the fireman, busy whirling the controls on the fire engine.

'The kitten. Look!' Tim held him up.

'Well, you wouldn't read about it. Must've jumped, all that way down.' The fireman stared at the kitten. 'Did you catch him?'

'Yes. I caught him, but . . .' Tim wanted to explain, to tell someone about his great feat.

'Well, wonders will never cease,' interrupted the fireman, jumping down from the truck and running back towards the fire.

Tim suddenly realized that this whole adventure must have taken rather a long time, and that he was expected home; so he ran off too, holding the kitten tightly in his arms.

Chapter 3

Steffy and Mum were sitting at the table with dinner plates in front of them when Tim burst in through the back door.

'Where on earth have you—' Tim's mother started, then, 'What is that?'

It might have seemed a queer question, since it was quite obviously a kitten that Tim still held in his arms, but he was too excited to notice.

'Mum, there was a fire. I climbed up on the roof and got him. Can we keep him, Mum? Please, please can we?'

Meanwhile Steffy had shot out of her chair and was stroking the kitten and crooning to it, 'Little kitty-cat, will you be my little cat?'

'What do you mean, a fire?' their mother was exclaiming at the same time. 'You didn't go near that burning warehouse in Barkly Street, Tim? That's so dangerous—'

'But I got the kitten, Mum. He would have been burnt. The firemen were too busy to save him.'

Their mother took the kitten gently. 'Let's have a look at him. He has been near a fire, too. You can smell the smoke on his fur. Tim, I don't know what you've been up to.'

'It's all right, Mum. I wasn't in any danger, really.'

'Well, wash your hands, quickly. Dinner's nearly cold. You too, Steffy.' Mum put the kitten down on an empty chair. 'Whatever are we going to do with him?'

'Can't we keep him, Mum?' Tim was washing his hands at lightning speed at the kitchen sink. 'I'll look after him, and feed him, and everything.'

'I don't know.' Their mother looked longingly at the kitten. 'We said we wouldn't get another cat after old Blackie died.'

'Please, Mum.'

'I'll think about it.' This was usually an encouraging reply. 'Anyway, he might belong to someone. We'd better put a notice up in the corner shop.'

After dinner, while Steffy was in the bath, Tim sat down at the table to write the notice. Suddenly, to his horror, he noticed that he was still wearing the Spiderman runners. In the confusion and excitement over the kitten, nobody had noticed. Quickly he slipped them off, fetched his sandals from outside, and stowed the runners safely in their box, back in his school bag. He took the lunchbox out and put it on the sink. Now Mum would have no reason to look in his bag. Then he sat down again. The kitten squeaked and tried to jump on to his lap, but it was too high. He reached down and scooped up the little furry bundle. The kitten curled up in his lap, purring loudly.

'Have you lost a little cat?' wrote Tim, painstakingly. He was not quite sure how to spell kitten. 'I found him in a fire in Barkly Street.'

'That's very good,' said his mother, coming into the room and reading over his shoulder. 'Now you'd better describe him.'

Tim looked doubtfully at the kitten. He was like a miniature tiger, with a complicated pattern of grey, black and white stripes.

'Just say he's a tabby,' advised his mother. Tim wrote it down. 'Now give our address and phone number.'

Tim wrote it down carefully, then put the notice in his school bag, ready to drop it off at the shop next morning. Meanwhile, his mother folded an old towel and put it in a corner of the kitchen. 'This can be a little bed for him,' she said. 'But don't get too attached to him, Tim. If someone turns up to claim him that's the end of it.'

Tim looked down at the kitten in his lap. It gazed back up at him, then shut its eyes and gave a big, contented smile.

Next morning Tim was up and dressed in record time. His mother and Steffy were both still asleep when he tiptoed down the stairs and into the kitchen. The kitten greeted him with shrill cries, and he poured some milk into its saucer and gave it the rest of the tin of tuna his mother had opened the night before. Then he started to assemble the makings of his own breakfast.

'I'll do that, Tim,' said his mother, coming into the kitchen as he was about to start. 'You might make a mess.'

30

'I wouldn't, Mum, really.'

'I may as well do it,' she said firmly, juggling bowls and packets at lightning speed. 'I'll make Steffy's at the same time. Daddy's going to ring this morning.' She set about arranging a tray.

'What time is it in Canada?'

'It'll be about five o'clock in the afternoon when he rings, but don't ask me what day it is, because I can never remember.'

'Will Daddy be at work?'

'Yes, love, you know the deal is that he rings from work and they pay for the call. It's part of his contract.'

'Mu-um,' came Steffy's wail from upstairs. 'Mummeeeeee.'

Mum sighed and headed upstairs with the tray.

In honour of the expected phone call, Tim went upstairs too, and dug out the Montreal Expos cap his father had sent, and put it on. The Expos were a top baseball team, his father had said. Tim felt good in the cap.

The phone call was exciting. Steffy monopolized the conversation at first, going into quite unnecessary details about her illness, but then Tim got his turn.

'It's snowing here, Tim,' said his father. 'They've had a snow plough clearing the street outside so that people can drive to work.'

'Maybe they could skate to work?'

'Some of them do – along the canal. It's actually faster than driving, at peak hour.'

'Wow.' Tim went off into a day-dream involving lots of ice and snow.

31

'Tim? You still there?' His father's voice broke through.

'Dad,' Tim took a deep breath. 'I climbed up a building. Straight up the side – like Spiderman.'

'That's nice.' His father didn't sound terribly impressed.

'There was a kitten on the roof, and there was a fire . . . Mum says we can keep the kitten if no-one claims it.'

'Well, you'll have to look after it, mate. Mum's got enough to do.'

Tim asked his usual question. 'When will you be home, Dad?'

'Won't be long. Another four weeks, mate.'

'You'll miss Steffy's birthday.'

'I know. Come on, now – where's your Mum?'

As Tim handed over the phone to his mother, he mouthed the words 'I'm going now'. She kissed him distractedly, her mind on the conversation. He grabbed his lunch off the kitchen bench and hurried out.

His first stop was the corner shop. Once he had made Mrs Pappas understand what he wanted, she was very kind, and lent him some sticky tape to attach his notice to the window. It looked fine there – but Tim hoped there would be no answer to it. He walked briskly off, carefully crossed the next two streets, rounded the corner, and he was in the shopping centre.

Only now did it occur to Tim that many shops would not be open yet. It was not even half-past eight. The newsagent and the milk-bar were doing business, but apart from a few shopkeepers washing windows and putting out their doormats, the rest of the street was deserted. However, it was possible that Mr Shy kept strange hours. Everything else about him was strange, after all.

Tim slowed down as he approached the antique shop. That was odd – he had thought Mr Shy's establishment was on this side of the shop. It must be on the other side. He walked on. No, the dress shop was on that side. He walked back. He felt sure now that this was where the doorway had been – but there was nothing. The hairdressers, which had always been there, was right next door to the antique shop. There was no space between – not a doorway, not a lane or an alley – nowhere he could look for Mr Shy. Tim went back past the antique shop and looked there again. No, there was just the dress shop, and the lady who ran it was now out the front, propping open her door. She looked at him strangely. Tim walked on quickly. He had a peculiar feeling, as though nothing was real any more – but the extra weight in his school bag reminded him that the Spiderman runners were still there, waiting to be worn.

Tim walked slowly the rest of the way to school, pondering. He had tried to give the runners back. He must have been mistaken about where the shop was. After school he would have a good look through the whole shopping centre. Mr Shy couldn't be far away. And meanwhile . . . a shiver of excitement ran through him. Meanwhile, there was the whole day at school, the Spiderman runners were in his bag, and there was nothing stopping him from having a last wear of them.

Tim stopped in the park and put the runners on, carefully packing away his sandals. The runners made his feet feel bouncy and springy, as though he wanted to run and jump all the time. The colours matched the red, white and blue of his Montreal Expos cap. He raced into the schoolyard and found Phillip.

'Where did you get them?' Phillip stared at the runners, his mouth open. 'They're fantastic.'

'I . . . sort of borrowed them, from a friend.' Tim found that these words just came out, unexpectedly. He had been going to tell Phillip about Mr Shy. 'The shoe shop ran out. I'll have to go back next week,' he went on.

'What about the five cents for the Matchbox catalogue?' demanded Phillip, waving it.

'Oh . . . I had to give Mum back the twenty dollars. I haven't got any money now.'

'Hmmm.' Phillip was gazing enviously at the shoes. 'Tell you what – if I can have a try of those runners I'll give you the catalogue for nothing.'

'I don't know . . .' Tim had an uneasy feeling about this suggestion. 'You take size four, don't you?'

'Oh, Mum just buys my shoes too big, so they'll last. I can squeeze into size three.'

'Well . . . all right.' Phillip was his best friend, and he'd been wanting that catalogue for ages.

Both boys sat down and took off their shoes. Phillip grabbed one of the Spiderman runners.

'Wow,' he said. 'Look at those laces!' He started to shove his foot into the shoe.

'Gee, it's tight!' he exclaimed. The more he

34

pushed to get his foot into the shoe, the harder he seemed to find it. It was as though the shoe was growing smaller. 'Are you sure it's size three?'

Tim looked all over the other shoe.

'It doesn't seem to have a size printed on it,' he said at last. 'But they fit me all right.'

'Well, I can't get it on.' Phillip tossed the shoe away in disgust.

'What about the catalogue?'

'Sorry, kid,' grinned Phillip, putting his own shoes back on. 'That's the way it goes.'

The bell rang, and Tim hurriedly put the Spider-man runners back on his own feet. One of the nice things about these runners was that he had found he could put them on in a flash – the laces seemed to tie themselves. He picked up his school bag and hurried into line with his class.

At lunchtime Tim and Phillip took their sand-wiches to the farthest corner of the park and lay under the trees. When you were their age you didn't have to stay in the schoolground all the time. The park was a lot more fun, with huge trees – though you weren't supposed to climb them – and lots of grass.

Tim and Phillip lay in the dappled shade of the biggest tree, eating and talking quietly. Suddenly a deeper shadow fell across them.

'I like your hat,' said a menacing voice. Tim's heart sank.

'Ah, get lost.' Phillip didn't even look up. Some-times the best way to deal with Colin Peters, the school bully, was to ignore him. Colin was only in Year Five, but he was big – across, as well as up and down – and he was used to getting his own way. Nobody liked him, but he didn't care. He surrounded himself with smaller boys, who were too scared not to be on his side, and went round annoying people. He usually left Phillip alone, because Phillip was nearly as big as he was, but he especially enjoyed tormenting Tim.

'Give us a lend,' Colin went on, snatching at Tim's hat. Tim ducked away.

'Leave him alone,' growled Phillip. But just then Ricky, a rat-like little boy with permanently scabby knees, one of Colin's more daring offsiders, darted in.

'Let's see yer Matchbox book,' he challenged, grabbing it from Phillip's hand and jumping away. With a roar of rage Phillip leaped up and gave chase. Phillip was bigger, but Ricky was fast on his feet. He kept up a good lead, weaving in and out of the trees. Meanwhile Colin, with an ugly smile, swept the Montreal Expos hat off Tim's head and threw it high up in the tree, where it caught on a branch and stayed. Then he rushed off to help Ricky.

At that moment the warning bell rang. They had five minutes to get back into the schoolyard and line up for afternoon class. Tim stood gazing up into the big tree in despair. No-one in his class had ever climbed it, except Tara, and she was away from school with chicken-pox. Phillip was preoccupied with his catalogue and anyway, he was a poor climber. Everyone else was heading back to the school gate.

Tim looked down at his Spiderman shoes. The

silvery laces twinkled. He looked around. Nobody was watching. He ran at the tree and started up it. The runners made him feel very safe, and gave him terrific speed, so that he was at the top in a flash. But he was surprised to find that there were plenty of hand-holds and foot-holds on the rough surface of the tree trunk. Coming down in particular, he almost felt he could have climbed the tree without the Spiderman runners.

Tim was the last into line, his cap proudly perched on his head. Phillip was towards the back too, very red in the face, clutching his rather crumpled Matchbox catalogue. He stared at Tim.

'I thought he threw it in the tree?' he whispered.

'I climbed up and got it down,' Tim whispered back.

Colin, in the Year Five line, was also staring in disbelief. Tim stuck his tongue out at him.

'Settle down, class,' Miss Barker said as they trooped into the room. 'We'll do some Creative Writing.'

Tim groaned as she handed round the exercise

books. Phillip rubbed his hands together. 'I'm going to write about the Swiss Alps,' he said. Phillip had been all round the world, and always had plenty of ideas for his stories.

'What'll I write about?' asked Tim.

'Oh . . . you know. Just something you did in the holidays,' said Phillip, his usual advice.

'But Tim . . .' Miss Barker was by their desk at that moment, handing out their books. 'No more about the Great Barrier Reef, or glass-bottomed boats, eh?'

Tim stopped in dismay, pencil poised in his hand. 'What can I write about, then?'

'How about an adventure?' suggested Miss Baker. 'Something you'd like to do?'

Tim gazed thoughtfully at her. Surely Mr Shy had said something rather like that. He had an idea.

'One day I saw a house on fire,' he wrote. 'Suddenly I heard a funny noise. It was a little kiten . . .'

'There are two t's in kitten,' said Miss Barker gently, stopping by his desk again. But she seemed pleased. Tim wrote busily. He decided not to include Mr Shy, so he made up an extra bit about finding the Spiderman runners inside a broken television set at the tip. But he described everything else exactly as it had happened. The story flowed from his pencil and filled the page.

After school, Phillip said, 'Are you walking down the street? I'll come with you.'

'How come?' asked Tim. Phillip lived in the opposite direction.

'I've got to meet my Mum. We're going into the City to buy a flute.'

'Are you going to learn to play the flute now?'

'Yeah. I'm so good at the piano they reckon I should learn something else as well.'

Tim was lost in admiration. It was a good thing Phillip was so bad at maths – otherwise he would be unbearable.

They walked together. As usual Phillip had plenty to say, and it seemed that every shop window was crowded with interesting items to be discussed, so any worries Tim may have had about Mr Shy, and the fact that he really should be searching for the shoe library, were pushed into the back of his mind.

However, when Phillip stopped outside the antique shop to exclaim over a black cloak with scarlet lining which graced the window, Tim got the surprise of his life. Next door, right where he remembered it being yesterday, and where it definitely had not been this morning, was Mr Shy's window. Tim stared, fascinated, while Phillip prattled on about Dracula and Transylvania. He took a few steps towards the window. It was just the same, except that the boots on display had been replaced by a beautiful pair of embroidered slippers with long pointed toes, curling upwards.

'Come on,' came Phillip's voice right behind him. 'What are you looking at the silly old hairdresser's for? There's nothing there.'

Phillip did not seem to notice the shoe library.

'I'd better move,' went on Phillip. 'Mum'll be at the bus stop by now.' He hurried off along the street. Tim followed.

At the bus stop, Phillip's mother was frantically waving. 'Come on! The bus is here!'

Phillip broke into a run and jumped on the bus after his mother. He poked his head out the door. 'See you tomorrow!' he shouted.

Tim waved, and stood watching until the bus was out of sight. Then he ran back to the shoe library.

Chapter 4

Mr Shy was behind the counter when Tim entered the shop. He was sitting on a high stool, sewing. When he saw Tim, he bundled up his work and shoved it under the counter, adjusting his glasses so that he could peer at Tim through the top pair.

'Excuse me,' Tim couldn't help asking. 'What was that you were making?'

'Just something for a friend,' said Mr Shy evasively.

'It looked . . . sort of like dolls' clothes,' Tim persisted.

'Curiosity killed the cat, boy,' said Mr Shy sternly. 'That's if the fire didn't, hee hee.' He wheezed horribly.

'How did you know about that?'

Mr Shy dug deep into his pockets and came up with a large watch on a silver chain, attached somewhere inside his clothing. He stared at it, then announced, 'Time's up. Down to business.'

'Well,' said Tim. 'I brought the shoes back.' He took them off and reached into his bag for the box and his own sandals.

'Sorry you couldn't keep them longer,' said Mr Shy.

'I would've brought them back this morning,'

Tim explained, putting on his sandals. 'But I couldn't find the shop.'

'That's right. You won't always find me here.'

'But it wasn't just you. The whole shop was . . . sort of . . . missing.'

'The shop's no use without me in it, is it boy?' wheezed Mr Shy. 'Just a waste of space. Now, what'll you have next?'

'Oh – I don't think I'd better borrow anything else,' said Tim firmly.

'Why's that?'

'Well . . . I might get into trouble.'

'I see. The Spiderman runners got you into trouble, did they?'

'Not really,' said Tim. 'Actually, they got me out of trouble at school today.'

'Hmm. But you didn't like the things that happened when you wore them?'

'Oh yes, I did. I saved the kitten, and . . .'

'Well, it's up to you, of course.' Mr Shy picked up the Spiderman runners and packed them into the box. Tim watched regretfully as they disappeared.

'You'd better go home, hadn't you?' said Mr Shy.

'Maybe . . . maybe I might borrow another pair of shoes,' ventured Tim.

'That's the spirit. What do you want to do – look in the catalogue, or just browse for a while?'

'I'm a bit late – what about those slippers in the window, with the curly toes?'

'Ah yes. You'll have fun with those. Word of advice, boy.' Mr Shy leaned on the counter and

42

contrived to peer at Tim through both pairs of glasses at once, giving him the appearance of having six eyes. 'If you get into deep water, take them off. Hmm? Take them off. That's the ticket.'

'I don't think I'll be going swimming in them,' said Tim, mystified.

'Not deep water, then. But if you get into a pickle, a jam, a stew—'

Tim found this prospect a bit alarming.

'You know what I mean,' went on Mr Shy, patiently. 'A hot seat, a sticky wicket . . . up the proverbial creek. Just remember – get 'em off, eh?'

'OK,' said Tim. He thought he understood. The bit about taking the shoes off was clear, anyway.

Tim took the slippers, which Mr Shy had packed into a box. Mr Shy wrote something on a card, which he had drawn from the gloomy recesses under the counter, and stamped it with a flourish.

'All right, boy. Off you go.'

'Goodbye. See you next time.'

When Tim stepped out the door the bright sunshine outside dazzled him for a moment. When his eyes were back to normal he turned to see if Mr Shy had replaced the window display. The shop had gone. Just as it had been this morning, there was nothing between the thrift shop and the hairdresser's. Tim hoisted his school bag on his back and ran all the way home.

At dinner that night Tim's mother was withdrawn and cross. Steffy was grumpy and refused to eat anything. Tim sat as quietly as he could and tried hard to remember his table manners. Afterwards, while Mum was washing up, he got out his books without being told and did his maths homework. His mother helped him.

'Is six fours twenty-two?' he would ask.

'Now, you've just worked out that five fours make twenty,' she reminded him. 'You have to add on another four, don't you?'

'Mum,' said Tim carefully, rubbing out his mistake. 'Are you worried about Steffy?'

'A bit,' she sighed. 'Her temperature should be down by now. I think she'd better sleep with me tonight. Maybe I won't have to get up so many times.'

'Are you tired?'

'Yes.' She smiled. 'I know I'm hard to get on with at the moment, Tim. I'm sorry. It's just . . . I am tired, I'm worried, and I miss Daddy.'

'It's good when he rings, though, isn't it?'

'Oh yes, but you can't say much in a phone call. And then – it's a whole week until he rings again.'

'When Daddy comes back, will he ever have to go away again?'

'Yes, Tim, I'm afraid that's his job. He's so good at setting up those wretched computers that he usually gets called in, sooner or later. And the wretched company is busily making sales all over the world.'

Tim picked up the kitten and stroked it behind the ears. 'Miss Barker says that if Daddy works with computers, he must be good at maths. She says I should be good at maths too.'

'You're all right at maths, Tim,' said his mother gently. 'You just have to learn your tables, and stop day-dreaming. Anyway, Daddy says working with computers doesn't have much to do with maths at all. It's more like solving puzzles, and riddles. And being resourceful.'

The kitten purred loudly and dug its claws into Tim's bare legs. He moved it into a more comfortable position.

'No-one's rung about him yet,' remarked Tim's mother.

'Can we keep him, then?' Tim looked up eagerly.

'We'd better wait a day or two more.'

Tim sighed. 'I wish Dad wasn't a Troubled Shooter.'

That was Steffy's term for their father's job, after she had heard him describe himself as a trouble-shooter. Tim always imagined his father shooting all over the place, unhappy at leaving his family behind.

'Well, someone's got to do the job he does. At least we'll have him home for a while this time.'

Tim finished his homework in silence and got himself ready for bed. While his mother was preoccupied with Steffy he quietly carried his school bag upstairs and put it under his bed. Then he went and lay on his parents' bed with the others while Mum read the bedtime story. It was only Little Red Riding Hood, but he liked to listen to her reading. Steffy dozed off before the story was over, and they tiptoed out of the room. Mum gave him a quick kiss goodnight and went off downstairs. Tim got into bed and turned on his reading light.

He picked up the book he was reading. He was

supposed to be doing a Book Review of it for school, but he hadn't got very far with it yet.

Under the bed, the Arabian slippers lay in their white box in his school bag.

Tim turned the page and looked at the picture. It wasn't a very exciting one. He flipped over the pages to see how many there were. There were quite a lot. He worked out in his head how much more he had to read to get halfway through the book. It was still quite a big number.

The slippers lay there, under the bed, curling up their toes.

Sighing, Tim put the book down and turned off his light. He could still see quite well in the light from the hall. The kitten strolled into his room, and curled up on a pile of discarded clothes, purring. Tim got out of bed and dragged out his school bag. He took out the slippers and examined them. They were soft and warm to the touch, embroidered with an intricate design in many dark, mysterious colours, but with silver and gold threads too, which picked up the faint light, and glowed. Tim sat down on the red patterned rug in the middle of the room, and put one of them on. Like the Spiderman runners it fitted perfectly, as if made for his foot.

The kitten bounded over to Tim and climbed on to his lap. He patted it gently with one hand, while with the other he put on the remaining slipper.

The rug quivered and started to shake. The kitten jumped off Tim's lap and stood stiff-legged beside him. Its tail went bushy, like a fox's. Tim grabbed the edge of the rug as it rippled and bulged, while the kitten pounced on the undulations. Then, slowly and ponderously, the rug lifted itself altogether off the floor and sailed out the open window and upwards, climbing steeply into the sky.

Tim clutched desperately at the upper edge of the rug as it rose at such a terrifying angle that he felt sure he might slide off at any moment. The kitten crawled as far under Tim as it could get, and clung on too. After a while the rug slowly levelled out, and Tim ventured to peep over the side. Far below he could see the twinkling lights of the city, hidden here and there by clouds. There were other clouds around him, looking like wisps of smoke; and far above was a velvety black sky, blacker than he had ever seen it, with millions of silvery stars and an enormous moon, almost completely full.

On sailed the rug, sometimes smoothly, sometimes rocking and bumping in the uneven air. The kitten, still burrowed under Tim, started to purr, and Tim dozed off. He awoke with a start to find the rug descending as steeply as it had risen. He was now in danger of plunging head first off it into the darkness below. Somehow, clinging on wherever he could, he managed to turn himself round and grab the back edge of the rug, which was now uppermost. During this manoeuvre the kitten crawled right inside Tim's pyjama top, where it nestled safely, if a little scratchily.

Once in a reasonably safe position, Tim glanced over his shoulder to see where the rug was taking him. Once more there were lights below, but fainter

and more scattered than those of the city he had just left. Against the sky, faintly illuminated by moonlight, he could sometimes make out the outlines of buildings; but they were not shaped like buildings he had seen, except in pictures. There were more curves than straight lines, with little balconies jutting out at odd angles here and there; and most of the roofs seemed dome-shaped, or starting off curved but then rising to a point. Lights flickered in a few windows, and it was towards a window in one of the largest buildings that the rug was headed. The window was wide open and a warm light glowed within as they swooped in and landed with a bump on a hard stone floor.

The landing knocked all the breath out of Tim, and it was a moment before he had recovered enough to look around. He was in a very large room, lit by a pair of tall brass lamps, like the ones that decorated the mantelpiece at Jonathon's house. Several rugs, rather like the one he had arrived on, were scattered over the floor, and some hung on the whitewashed walls. There was no furniture, apart from what appeared to be a bed on a platform at one end of the room, draped with patterned cloth, and a large, ornately carved box. Before Tim had really had time to take in the scene, a man hurried into the room.

'Master, Master!' cried the new arrival, wringing his hands at the sight of Tim. 'It's almost dawn. I thought you were dressing yourself for the ceremony!'

His words sounded odd, as though he were talking another language; but it couldn't have been that, because Tim understood him well enough. Stranger still was his appearance: his black eyes and pointed black beard below a great turban fastened with a glittering jewel, his embroidered tunic falling below his knees, his baggy trousers and, not least, his slippers, which curled upwards at the toes, just like Tim's, though not quite as ornate.

Without wasting any more breath on his reproaches, the man had dived into the big box and was rummaging around in it. Clothes flew out in all directions. 'All white, I think,' he muttered. 'Here, put this on.'

A white satin tunic landed next to Tim. The kitten pounced on it.

'And these . . .' A pair of white baggy trousers

49

followed the tunic. They looked a little easier to manage, so Tim clambered into them. Meanwhile, his companion approached with a long white cloth. 'The tunic first,' he muttered, taking off Tim's pyjama top and tossing it on to the rug. The kitten jumped on to it and began kneading it with his claws.

'Excuse me,' Tim managed, as he struggled into the tunic. 'What am I getting dressed up for?'

'Poor child,' said the man, as his fingers flew over the intricate fastenings. 'You've been sleeping.'

He finished the tunic and began to wind the cloth around Tim's head.

'I know,' said Tim cautiously. 'I . . . I've forgotten why I'm here.'

'You are to see the Grand Vizier, to put your father's case.'

'My father?'

'Abou Ben Mori Sun.' The man touched his forehead and lips in a gesture of reverence as he said the name. Tim was startled. His father's name really was Ben Morrison.

'What must I say to the Grand Vizier?' he asked.

'Whatever is in your heart,' said his new friend mysteriously, as he fastened Tim's turban with a deep red jewel. 'But if you command me I will explain the problem to him,' he added helpfully.

'All right,' said Tim, 'I command you.'

To his astonishment the man bowed so low his nose almost touched the floor.

'Whatever my honoured Master wills,' he murmured.

To hide his confusion Tim went over and stroked

the kitten, which had curled up on his pyjama top. His companion straightened up and said cautiously, 'We are expected, Highness. The Grand Vizier grows troublesome if he is kept waiting.'

'All right, then. Let's go.'

Chapter 5

Tim followed his awesome new friend out the door and through a maze of narrow passageways and winding stairs. Sometimes they went up, sometimes down, until finally they emerged in a large hall draped with shimmering cloths. At the far end was an arched doorway guarded by two enormous dark men with bare tops and billowing trousers, each with a brilliantly jewelled belt from which hung a wicked-looking curved sword. As Tim and his companion appeared, they drew these swords in perfect unison and crossed them over the doorway. Surprisingly, Tim's companion seemed less afraid of them than he was of Tim himself.

'Make way for Tariq Ibn Mori Sun,' he growled. Instantly they dropped their swords and bowed low. Tim and his companion passed into a room of dazzling magnificence.

The ceiling was so high you could barely see it, and was hung with clouds of silky white fabric. The walls, broken at intervals by high pointed windows, were richly patterned in many dark colours, outlined with silver. An enormously long red carpet led from where Tim stood to the far end of the room and up some stairs to a platform on which stood a glittering golden throne, studded with jewels. No-one sat there, but on a lower platform, to one side, was another throne, silver where the first had been gold, and this one was surrounded by people and inhabited by a withered little man with a stringy grey beard and a great hooked nose beneath two glittering black eyes.

Obviously this was the person they had come to see, the Grand Vizier. Tim walked as steadily as he could towards him. He felt that his companion would be disappointed if he showed any sign of being afraid in these strange surroundings, so he had made up his mind to appear braver than he actually felt.

'Your Excellency,' began Tim's companion, when they were within earshot. 'May I present his Highness Tariq Ibn Mori Sun, first-born son of the rightful ruler of this land.'

'Ha.' The Grand Vizier was not apparently impressed. 'And how may I know it is he?'

Red-ribboned scrolls were produced, unrolled and examined by a group of old men, with much muttering and glancing towards Tim. Finally the oldest man whispered something in the ear of the Grand Vizier, whose expression grew blacker than ever at the news.

'And so, stripling,' he said. 'Where hides your father, that he must send a child to put his claim?'

'If it pleases Your Excellency,' put in Tim's companion respectfully. Tim could feel that he was trembling, but he did not seem afraid. 'My most exalted Master had started forth on the road to this palace when he was set upon by brigands who murdered most of his party, and injured him so terribly that anyone might think he must die too. But my Master has the strength of a thousand lions, and the physicians say he will live, though his recovery must be slow. Time grows short, and the third full moon comes tomorrow night, when the matter must be completed. Therefore my young Master has come to put his father's claim, according to the rules set down in the thirteenth volume of the Golden Book.'

The Grand Vizier turned to Tim. 'And what say you, young prince?'

Tim was terror-struck at the obvious seriousness of the situation, and at the way in which all eyes turned to him to hear his answer, but to his surprise he opened his mouth and words came out.

'My father is the rightful ruler of all this land,' he declared. 'And I am his heir and successor. I will carry out the Task and thus claim the throne in my father's name by moonrise tomorrow.'

This seemed to be the right answer, and the old men immediately went into a huddle again. After a few minutes one of them emerged and struck a silver gong. Before its note had finished echoing through the room, two large black men, bare from the waist up like the guards, came trotting into the room, carrying between them a draped table on which stood a large glass ball on a stand. They set this down before the silver throne and the old men surrounded it, muttering and mumbling. Then the oldest one turned to the Grand Vizier and announced, 'The Task!'

The Grand Vizier shifted his gaze and smiled, a horrid smile which revealed a mouthful of gold

teeth. Tim turned to see what had pleased his enemy so much. The old men had drawn back, revealing the glass ball. It seemed to have turned itself into a sort of round television set, and in it could be seen a tall and spindly castle clinging to a craggy mountain, with steep cliffs dropping away on all sides. It must have been very high up, because the uppermost towers were lost in dark clouds. Around and around the castle flew the hideous shapes of many dragons. They were not brightly coloured like the dragons in pictures, but black, except when smoke poured from their flaring nostrils and their mouths spat brilliant flames. The castle was dark except for a single light burning in a high window, and Tim thought he could make out the shape of someone sitting there.

Tim's companion stepped forward. 'Objection to the Task,' he announced. 'The Dragons' Dungeon is many days' journey from here. It cannot be done within the time.'

'Objection overruled,' purred the Grand Vizier. 'If your Master is truly of the royal blood he will find a way. Announce the Task!' This was directed at the oldest of the old men, who now stepped forward.

'Witness the last surviving member of the family of the former Shah,' he intoned. 'The Princess Yasmin is a prisoner of the Dragons and must be rescued before the full moon, when they will kill and eat her.'

'It will be done,' said Tim's companion through gritted teeth, and stalked from the room. Tim tried to stalk after him in a similar fashion, but he had to run a few steps to keep up. Tim's companion looked very grave as they made their way back to his room.

'Why was the Grand Vizier so . . . so . . . unfriendly?' Tim wanted to know.

'Poor child.' His companion gazed at him, and sighed. 'You must know how the Grand Vizier hates you and all your family, and how he will do whatever he can to prevent you from winning the throne.'

'Why?'

'Because the law states that if your family fails, he must take the throne himself.' He grew angry, and his dark eyes blazed. 'How it stuck in my throat to tell him of brigands attacking your father! He knew very well, since he arranged it himself. No doubt the so-called brigands all lie in a ditch with their throats cut by now, for failing to kill my most beloved Master.' His eyes were filling with tears. Tim hastened to change the subject.

'Can you help me rescue this princess?' he asked.

'No, little Master. No man may help the Doer of the Tasks.'

'And do you think I could do it by myself?' asked Tim.

'Oh, my poor little Master. No-one has ever entered the Dragons' Dungeon and lived to tell the tale. Besides, it is far from here. You'd have to climb those barren mountains, which the dragons continuously watch. Even your father could not do it. We must find a place of safety and live out our lives in exile.'

They entered Tim's room in gloomy silence. His companion started picking things up and putting them in the box.

'What will happen to the Princess, then?' asked Tim.

'You heard.'

'Oh.'

'And who gave your cousin to the dragons in the first place, I'd like to know?' muttered Tim's companion savagely as he worked, now stripping the covers off the bed.

'Is she my cousin?' Somehow this made the

thought of the Princess being eaten by dragons even worse.

'Of course. You are the last of the royal family.'

Tim sat down on the rug in the middle of the room. Everything seemed to be whirling around inside his head. Under him the rug quivered, as it had done back in his bedroom. It seemed eager to be moving. The slippers glittered on Tim's feet. One of them was pinching his toes a little, and he reached down to take it off, but then he stopped and looked up at his mournful companion.

'I'm going to try to do the Task,' he announced.

'But Master—'

'You are my servant, aren't you?' Tim demanded.

'Of course, but—'

'Then do as I say. Leave me, and don't come back until tomorrow morning.'

His companion bowed low and left the room in silence, but Tim could see his black eye a moment later, peering through the keyhole. Tim threw open the door.

'Away!' he commanded, trying to sound like Miss Barker at her worst.

The man scurried to the far end of the corridor, bowing all the way, and Tim returned to his room and picked up the kitten.

'We're in this together I think, kitty,' he murmured.

Then he sat down on the rug. It started to buckle and shake.

'Rug,' said Tim. 'I hope you know what you're doing. Take me to the Dragons' Dungeon.'

The rug lifted itself and swooped out the window,

straight into the sun, which by now was high in the sky. Tim stretched out, holding on to the edge, and the kitten crept into its customary position underneath him. The rug whirled along at dizzying speed. It was warm, and again Tim dozed off.

An icy wind that chilled him through his light clothing woke him. They were flying between the peaks of tall, ice-capped mountains. The sun had dropped, and the sky was a pale mauve colour. Straight ahead in the shadows was the castle Tim had seen in the glass ball. There were no dragons to be seen as they sped towards it, and Tim's spirits lifted. This was going to be easy. Then he heard a peculiar whirring noise, and the next minute a dragon swooped over him, its claws grazing his back as Tim dived to avoid it. The dragon was huge, its wingspan twice as wide as Tim's rug, and it smelt foul. Its wings were a ragged, dusty black, and its wicked eye glittered in the fading light. Before Tim had time to consider the danger he was in, another dragon swept at him from a different angle, searing him with its breath. He clung on to the rug as it ducked and weaved. He wished he had a weapon. Another dragon was coming straight at him, head on. He whipped off his turban and swiped at it. The turban came undone and a loop of material caught on the dragon's wing. The dragon jerked, nearly pulling Tim's arms out of their sockets. He let go the turban and the dragon, its wing now useless, plummetted shrieking towards the ground far below.

'Yippee!' cried Tim, dancing on the rug. The kitten hissed and spat over his shoulder. Turning, he saw another dragon racing in, and he dropped flat on the rug just in time as its fiery breath roared over him. The rug, with Tim and the kitten clinging to it with all their might, turned sharply and shot in through the single lighted window of the castle.

Tim hit the floor with a thud. For a moment he couldn't move. He saw a pair of feet clad in slippers like his own, then the voluminous folds of a silken skirt, into which the kitten rushed to hide itself, meowing. Tim's eyes slowly travelled upward to see that the dress belonged to a small girl, about his age, with very long black hair, smooth olive skin and a pair of almond-shaped eyes which were staring at him in horror.

'What are you doing here?' cried this vision, wringing her hands. 'They said a warrior would come to rescue me. Is this their idea of a joke?'

Tim was trying to think of a sharp reply when his eyes travelled upward still, beyond the girl to the window. A shadow darkened the room, and a bigger dragon than all the others landed on the windowsill, clinging on with its wicked talons. The Princess buried her face in her hands as it opened its mouth. All Tim could think of was water, and how he would like a big bucketful to throw into that hideously yawning face. Hadn't Mr Shy said something about . . . 'Deep Water', that's what he had said. The dragon took a deep breath and smoke from its nostrils filled the room. Tim reached down and tore off his shoes.

Chapter 6

Everything went black. Tim heard the roar of flames and someone screaming, but very far away, very faint. Around him everything was quiet, and dark, and still. He lay where he was, warm and comfortable, and closed his eyes.

'Tim!' A gentle voice penetrated the silence, and a hand grasped his shoulder. Tim opened his eyes a little. Sunlight outlined the curtains of his room, and he saw his mother's face. 'It's nearly nine o'clock,' she was saying. 'You've never slept in this late before.'

Tim sat up, bewildered. 'What about school?'

'It's Saturday!' his mother laughed.

'Oh. Yeah.' Tim thought for a minute. He had put the slippers on on Friday night, but he had spent at least a whole day . . . 'Isn't it Sunday?'

'No, Saturday. Come downstairs and have some breakfast. Steffy's been up for hours.'

When she had gone Tim looked around the room. The red rug was back in its normal position – a bit crooked, maybe. He peeped under the bed, dragged out his school bag and looked inside. The slippers were there, packed into their box. He was about to put them away again when something made him raise one to his nose. It smelled smoky.

Downstairs, his mother had made cheese on toast for him. Steffy was sitting at the kitchen table, drawing.

'My temperature's gone, Tim,' she said.

She did look a lot better. Her cheeks were not as red as before, and she had no new spots. Their mother was obviously pleased. She hummed to herself as she ran water into the sink and started clattering the dishes. Tim gloomily ate his toast.

'You're very quiet,' his mother remarked. 'Still a bit sleepy?'

'Mmmm.'

'Nothing wrong, is there?' she persisted.

'No. Just had a bad dream. A bit scary.' Tim shuddered as he thought of those dragons. But it wasn't even that, not really. He kept seeing the Princess, wringing her hands. Maybe if he'd stayed . . .

'By the way,' his mother's voice intruded on his thoughts, 'I haven't seen the kitten this morning. Did he sleep in your room?'

Tim stared at her.

'I thought I saw him heading upstairs,' she went on. 'Didn't he come in to you?'

'I . . . I don't know.'

'Oh, well. He might turn up. Pity if he has wandered off – I was getting quite attached to him.'

The day passed in a daze for Tim. After breakfast he went searching and calling for the kitten, but he knew it was no good. He went as far as the building where he had first found the little creature, half-expecting it to look like new again and the whole

62

adventure, kitten and all, to have been a dream. But the building stood, a blackened shell, still with the sharp smell of smoke hanging about it.

When he came home, with no kitten, Steffy cried. It took the two of them a long time to comfort her.

In the afternoon, while Steffy was resting and their mother was sewing in the front room, Tim got out his book on dragons. He had always loved the book, but now he read it with critical eyes.

For a start, all the dragons were in beautiful bright colours, with fancy patterns of scales on their backs – nothing like the real dragons he had seen, black and menacing, with their little red eyes and wings tattered from many battles. And then the tips on how to kill dragons, which he had hopefully turned to, were all very silly things where you tricked the dragon. You gave it some curry to eat so that it would have a drink of water and put out its own fire; or you painted a window on a brick wall and got the dragon to crash into it – things like that. The dragons Tim had seen wouldn't be fooled for a second.

Then he looked through his book on knights and castles. This was a bit more like it. Determined-looking knights, well protected by their chain-mail, waved heavy double-edged broadswords with both hands as they charged on horseback at the snarling dragons. Other knights practised their fighting skills with needle-sharp lances. You could almost hear the thunder of hooves as they flew at each other over the bright green grass. The book also showed pikes with long handles, and spike-studded balls on strings which you could whirl around over your head and let fly at the enemy. Tim liked the look of the short swords, which you could use with one hand, while holding a nice big shield with the other. He turned the page, and his heart sank. Here were pictures of some of the weapons being made. Men in leather aprons wielded huge hammers as they pounded the red-hot iron into shape. Behind them on the walls hung other mysterious-looking tools. Tim thought of the hammer and saw and the few odd bits of wood that were in his garden shed.

Next, he read with interest of how King Arthur's sword Excalibur was made for him by the Lady of the Lake. King Arthur, still only a boy, had walked down to the water's edge and a hand had appeared, waving the sword, its hilt afire with strange jewels that caught the evening light. There was another sword, too, which Arthur had pulled from a stone, thus proving himself to be King.

But there were no swords in stones anywhere around that Tim had seen, and he didn't think Sydney Harbour was the right sort of lake.

Even if he could arm himself with the right sort of weapon, Tim knew that he would have little chance of using it effectively against the dragons. There was a lot in the book about the skills involved in using these weapons, which the knights all started to learn in early childhood. He didn't have that much time.

A thought struck Tim and he ran downstairs to find his mother.

'Is it nearly full moon?' he asked.

'Yes, I think it is. It was pretty bright last night.' She looked at him thoughtfully. 'What's on your mind today, Tim?'

'Nothing.' Tim looked as innocent as he could.

'Hmm. Well, have a look at the calendar. I think it shows the phases of the moon.'

Tim looked. The full moon was tonight.

By bedtime, Tim's thoughts on the whole problem were clear. He had only two choices: to go back and try to rescue the Princess and the kitten, or not to go back. And he only had one weapon, a weapon which he did not really know how to use, but which might serve him better than all the broadswords and shields in the world. That weapon was magic.

Chapter 7

Steffy was back in her own bed that night. Tim lay rigid while she whispered to her dolls and sang little songs to herself. He decided to tell their mother that Steffy shouldn't have afternoon sleeps, even if she was sick.

'Are you awake, Tim?' she whispered a couple of times. Tim lay very still and tried to make his breathing slow, like a sleeping person. Downstairs he could hear the faint hum of the television.

At last Steffy was quiet. Tim waited. She turned over a few times in her bed, with little sighs. Finally he could hear her breathing evenly. He counted the breaths. At fifty he was still not sure, so he counted on. A hundred breaths.

Tim slipped out of his bed and drew out his school bag. He took the slippers in his hands and looked uncertainly at the rug. He didn't really want to approach the dragons' strong-hold by air again, but on the other hand if he didn't use the rug he might end up somewhere else. He wished there was someone he could ask. Maybe if he waited until he saw Mr Shy again . . .

Sighing, Tim sat down on the rug, took a deep breath and put on both slippers together.

Unconsciously, he had closed his eyes. This time

66

the rug did not lift off the floor, but seemed to spin where it was, faster and faster. When Tim opened his eyes bright lights flashed at him, so he screwed them shut again. After a moment the rug slowed down, then stopped.

He looked up. He was in the same position as the previous night, lying face down on the floor in the Princess's room. She was staring at him with wide eyes, and the kitten was peeping round from behind her skirts, staring too. The dragon had gone from the windowsill, and outside it was dark.

'How did you do that?' gasped the Princess, kneeling down and reaching out fearfully to touch him.

'Do what?' asked Tim, sitting up.

'You disappeared. I thought the dragon's fire was so strong it had burnt you up to nothing. And now, hours later, here you are again!'

'Where are the dragons?' asked Tim.

'Somewhere out there.' She shuddered. 'At night they go hunting, but a few stay to guard the castle. Look.'

Together they went to the window and cautiously peeped out. Tim realized now that the light was out in the Princess's room, but the bright moonlight had enabled them to see each other. Outside, the jagged outlines of the mountains were dark against the silvery sky. For a while everything was silent and still, then a familiar hum made them duck their heads. The shadow of a dragon swept across them as it flapped past the window.

'How many?' whispered Tim.

'Two, I think. The others won't be back until morning.' She looked at Tim. 'Why on earth did you come?'

'Well . . . to rescue you, of course.'

'That's ridiculous. I'm supposed to be rescued by a great warrior, with armour, and weapons, and . . . and . . . well, someone the dragons would take seriously.'

'Sorry,' said Tim angrily. 'The warriors were all too busy. Anyway, I've killed one dragon already.'

Yasmin didn't seem terribly impressed. She paced around the room for a while, then sat down on the bed, gazing into space. To Tim's annoyance the kitten jumped on to her lap and nestled in.

'Look.' said Tim. 'You can sulk if you like, but I'm more interested in getting out of here. Are you coming with me?'

Yasmin looked at him with her liquid eyes. Maybe she was a nice person underneath, Tim thought. Just badly brought up, his mother would have said.

'Not now,' she said. 'We'd never get past the patrols. But there is one chance. In the last hour before dawn – between moonset and sunrise – it will be very dark.'

'Great!' said Tim. 'That's when we'll go.'

He looked across the room. 'You haven't got any broadswords or anything, have you?'

The Princess laughed. 'It wouldn't help if I had. Have you ever tried to lift a broadsword?'

They passed the rest of the night quietly playing with the kitten and watching the progress of the moon as it sank slowly towards the western peaks.

Sometimes one of them would doze off. Tim began to worry that they might both fall asleep and miss their chance to leave, so he started talking, telling Yasmin about his school, his friends, his Lego spaceship, his cousin Jason's feats on his skateboard (except that Tim gave the impression that they were *his* feats). Princess Yasmin laughed and laughed. The more he talked, the more she laughed. Sometimes Tim tried to stop, fearing that the noise might attract the dragons, but each time she begged him to continue. Even talk of school and Miss Barker entertained her, and when he got on to computers and his father's job she could hardly contain herself.

'I always knew Uncle Ben was a magic user!' she breathed. 'Can he really put all the wisdom of the world into a box?'

'Yes – sort of.' Tim thought he had explained that rather well.

'Oh, isn't he wonderful!' said Yasmin. 'I wish he had come to rescue me.'

'I can do things on computers too,' said Tim defensively. 'And I'm not bad at school. Miss Barker says I'm getting good at stories.'

'You are, you are!' agreed Yasmin. 'One of my slaves, Scheherezade, tells lovely stories; but yours are even better.'

As the time to depart came closer, Tim explored the room. There was not much there, but remembering how cold it was outside he stripped the covers off the bed. The Princess took a shawl which was hanging on a hook and wrapped it around herself. She tied the ends firmly around her waist and

69

tucked the kitten into it. He peeped out, his ears twitching.

The moon dropped out of sight. Immediately, darkness flooded the room.

'This is it,' murmured Tim. He tossed the bed-covers on to the rug and took Yasmin's hand. Together they stepped on to the rug and lay face-down. 'Don't forget, rug,' he said. 'Evasive action, right?'

The rug shook itself impatiently and took off. They soared through the window, a blacker shadow against the black sky. The rug raced along. Suddenly it banked and swerved to one side.

'Hey!' muttered Tim, grabbing for the edge. Then his heart sank as he felt a cold draught swishing across his face, and heard the flap of a dragon's wing. He hadn't even seen it coming, but now a shadow against the far-off stars showed him that another was diving at them from the opposite side.

'Keep down, Yasmin!' he yelled, and the rug tilted off to the other side. But Yasmin was on her feet holding one of the blankets. As the dragon swooped over them, missing by inches, she threw the blanket over its head. The rug seemed to drop away from under them as it dived, and they threw themselves down on it, clutching at the billowing edges. Then Tim jumped up again, snatching at the other blanket. The first dragon they had seen was coming in now, roaring smoke and flames. Tim waved the blanket in front of himself, bullfighter style. The dragon charged, and at the last moment Tim skipped away, leaving it, too, entangled in a blanket. The rug dipped again, and the two dragons

70

could be seen, one on either side, struggling fiercely with their now-smouldering blankets. Then, to Yasmin's horror, Tim jumped up again.

'Here I am!' he shouted. 'Come and get me!'

The enraged dragons wheeled in the sky and plunged at the sound. Tim dropped to his stomach.

'Up this time, rug,' he whispered. The rug shot upwards and the two dragons, diving simultaneously for the spot just below where they had last heard Tim's voice, collided with a crash and a roar that shook the encircling mountains. Screaming and slashing, each one still blinded and obviously thinking it was attacking Tim at last, they dropped together out of sight.

The rug sailed on. Tim lay still, puffed out. The Princess lay beside him.

'We did it, Tariq!' she said, her eyes shining. 'It was a Task, wasn't it?'

'Sure was!' grinned Tim.

'I can't wait to see the Grand Vizier's face,' she said with satisfaction. 'He took me to the dragons, you know. And he told them you were coming – that's why there were so many of them guarding the castle last night. Just wait until Uncle Ben is King! He'll have him drawn and quartered, at the very least.'

'Just what does that mean?' Tim had always wanted to know.

'Haven't you ever seen it?' She was surprised. 'First they cut them in two from the top of the head downwards. That's the drawing part. Then they chop the bits in halves across the middle. Quarters, you see?'

Tim didn't much like the sound of that, even for the Grand Vizier, but he thought it best to say nothing.

The rug sailed on smoothly. It seemed to travel more slowly with two passengers, not counting the kitten; and the sun climbed high in the sky and dropped in the west as they drifted over a patchwork of forests, open green fields, sandy desert, rivers and lakes. Yasmin slept for much of the day, but Tim stayed awake, watching for familiar sights.

He was very hungry, and the kitten was mewing piteously. But more than that, he was worried. Behind them, the sun was dropping out of the sky. Moonrise, the old men had said; but a full moon rises almost immediately after sunset. Tim knew that from a very scary movie about vampires he had watched once, while staying with Auntie Marjorie.

The gold of the sinking sun was reflected on the walls of the palace when at last Tim and Yasmin found themselves floating gently in through the window. The door was open and Tim's companion stood there, his mouth hanging open in astonishment.

'Master . . .' he stammered.

'Don't ask,' interrupted Tim, very pleased with himself. 'Let's just go to the throne room. Quick!'

The sky was blood-red through the pointed windows and servants were passing through the corridors, lighting the lamps, as they ran up and down staircases and through echoing corridors to the throne room. At the sight of Yasmin the Grand

Vizier fainted away. The old men lined up in front of Tim, and the oldest one of all intoned: 'Have you completed the Task, O Wanderer?'

'I have,' replied Tim proudly.

The old man turned to Yasmin. 'I ask you as witness, O Daughter of the Royal House. Did the Wanderer receive help in completing the Task?'

'No, Great and Wise One,' Yasmin replied respectfully.

The old men then all together knelt and kissed the ground in front of Tim. Musicians raced in and struck up a merry tune. Soon everyone was dancing – everyone except the Grand Vizier, who had recovered enough to stagger from the room on the shoulders of a couple of muttering cronies.

Trays of food began circulating, and Tim reached eagerly for some. There were piles of rice sweetened with raisins, lots of something very like Lebanese bread, which was one of Tim's favourite foods, with things to dip it in, including the fishy pink stuff that Steffy adored. There were lots of sticky cakes with nutty green fillings, and all sorts of fruit, some of which Tim had never seen before. It seemed that everyone was laughing and talking at once, and Tim's companion was drinking copious quantities of a colourless liquid from something that looked like the vase on Auntie Marjorie's mantelpiece.

Yasmin, like Tim, was following the food trays around, eating for all she was worth. Tim caught up with her in a quiet corner.

'You really did help me,' he said. 'You didn't have to be modest when they asked.'

'Shhh,' she said. 'They mightn't count the Task if they hear about all those dragons I killed.'

'All those what—!' But Tim saw his favourite cakes passing in the distance, and he ran to get one.

Later, he came upon his companion, reclining on some embroidered cushions.

'Don't get up,' said Tim hastily. His companion still struggled to find his feet.

'I ORDER you not to get up,' said Tim. The man sank thankfully into his cushions. 'I just want to know. Would they really not count the Task if Yasmin helped me?'

'They might not, Master. The rules say that no man may help you.'

'Yasmin's not a man,' laughed Tim.

'It means no person, that rule. They just say man.'

'Well they should say what they mean,' said Tim sternly. 'When my Dad's King you can tell him to change that.'

When he had had enough to eat Tim slipped out, unnoticed. He ran upstairs to his room and fetched the kitten. He was pleased and proud to have won the throne, but as far as he was concerned Abou Ben Mori Sun, whoever he was, could have it. Tim had had enough of this place where your friends kissed your feet and your enemies set dragons on to you. Holding the kitten under one arm, he gently drew off his slippers.

Chapter 8

Tim awoke to find Steffy sitting on the end of his bed, the purring kitten in her arms.

'Look, Tim! He's back. Mum says we'll never know where he's been.'

Tim patted the kitten's head, and it smiled at him in its mysterious way. Once more Tim had slept very late. He expected to feel tired after the adventures of the last two nights, but all he felt was very hungry, in spite of all those nutty green cakes. As a special treat his mother agreed to let him make his own breakfast, even including a boiled egg. Tim ate and ate, while Steffy stood on a stool and washed the dishes, chattering all the time.

'Mum says we can keep kitty. It's been three days and no-one's come for him.'

'That's great!' Tim looked up, smiling. 'We'll have to think of a name for him.'

'Well, I think he should be called Chicken-pox,' said Steffy firmly. 'And he can share my bed and play with my toys.'

'I don't know about Chicken-pox,' said their mother doubtfully, coming into the room. 'Why don't we call him Phoenix?'

'What does that mean?' asked Tim.

'It's a bird in a story. The Phoenix was in a fire, but it rose from the ashes – you know, it didn't die. Our kitten's a bit like that. He still smells of smoke, have you noticed?'

Tim could think of a good reason for that, but he didn't mention it. Instead, he said, 'Feenix. Hmm. How do you spell it?'

'P-H-O-E ...'

'Oh Mum, that's too complicated. Let's wait until we think of something really terrific.'

'OK. And he's not sleeping in your bed, Steffy.'

The day passed very pleasantly. They drove out to Auntie Marjorie's for the day. Luckily her children had had chicken-pox. Steffy was much better, and became ecstatic when her cousin Helen took her for a ride on her pony. Jason, who was twelve, took Tim to the BMX bike track and taught him quite a few new tricks. Tim couldn't exactly do any of them, but he watched Jason carefully and listened to all his advice. He longed to tell Jason how he had killed three dragons, but he guessed Jason would take a bit of convincing, and he didn't want to be accused of telling lies.

Auntie Marjorie was known as a good cook, so her lunches were sometimes rather alarming; but today there was a delicious chicken soup, with plenty of icecream afterwards. Tim had to lie down for a while on the couch. He heard his mother and Auntie Marjorie talking quietly as they washed the dishes.

'What's to *stop* you getting a job?' Auntie Marjorie was saying. 'You can't manage two children and a mortgage on one income, even a good one like Ben's.'

'Oh, I don't know. Maybe when the children are old enough,' his mother replied.

'They're old enough now. You baby them too much, Annie. Let them stand on their own two feet.'

Hear, hear, thought Tim sleepily.

On Monday and Tuesday Steffy was still at home, although she didn't seem to be sick at all, and Tim was able to walk to and from school by himself. He kept the curly-toed slippers ready in his bag, but Mr Shy was not there. He was not there on Wednesday, either, when the three of them walked past on the way to school. Steffy was now completely recovered. Her spots were fading and, armed with flowers and drawings for her teacher, she skipped along eagerly. Tim re-entered an old argument with his mother.

'Mum, you don't have to walk to school with us. I could look after Steffy.'

'I'm just not sure, darling. She's a bit of a handful.'

'She'd be all right with me, Mum. She's sensible about crossing roads now.'

'I know, but . . . Maybe after her birthday, when she's six.'

'You said that about *my* last birthday.'

'Just wait, love.'

Tim sighed. He never got anywhere in these discussions.

After school he came rushing out to meet his mother in the playground.

'Did you bring the money, Mum?'

78

'Of course.' She smiled. 'I thought you'd never come out.' Steffy was already out of her class, playing with her friends. Tim's class were the last ones out.

'I know. Miss Barker kept telling us to be quiet, and people kept talking and talking.'

'Well, let's go. I might get some shoes for Steffy too.'

The man in the shoe shop didn't seem to remember Tim but yes, he said, they had got some more Spiderman runners. Tim watched anxiously as he rummaged through the shelves, while behind him his mother and Steffy argued on and on about a pair of shoes Steffy had set her heart on, which Mum thought were 'not suitable'. Finally the man produced the right box with the right shoes in the right size. Tim tried them on. They were perfect – as ordinary Spiderman runners went. They didn't have any magic powers, but at least they were his, and at least he could be sure they were not going to take him off on any wild adventures.

Steffy was mollified with a pair of pink ballet slippers, and they left the shop. Tim was busy negotiating with his mother for the five cents change – he still wanted that Matchbox catalogue of Phillip's – as they walked down the street, when out of the corner of his eye he noticed it. Mr Shy's shop was back in its usual place.

This created a problem which Tim had not foreseen. If the shoe library was there he really should go into it; but he couldn't let Mum and Steffy know. They walked past, Tim trailing behind a little, looking desperately at Mr Shy's

79

window. The display today was a beautiful pair of ice skates, and Tim gazed longingly at them. Just then, as luck would have it, Mr Shy himself appeared in the window, making some small adjustment to the display. Tim jumped up and down, waving, and caught his eye. Then, pulling faces in the direction of his mother and Steffy, Tim mouthed the words 'I'll come tomorrow'. Mr Shy waved, appearing to understand. 'Tomorrow,' Tim mouthed again. He turned away, and saw his mother staring back at him.

'What on earth are you doing, Tim?'

'Oh . . . um . . . mouth exercises.'

'Mouth exercises?'

'For Choir. Miss Harris says I don't open my mouth wide enough.'

'She should see you at home.'

The next day Tim was up and dressed earlier than he had ever been before. While his mother was pre-occupied with doing Steffy's hair he said casually, 'Can I go now, Mum? I'm ready.'

'We won't be long, Tim.'

'I know, but I'd really like to be early. Phillip's bringing the Matchbox catalogue . . .'

'Oh, all right. Be careful crossing the road.'

Tim hurried through the shopping centre, only to be disappointed. Mr Shy was not there. Tim tried closing his eyes and opening them again. The shop was still not there. He tried turning his back, then quickly jumping around again, as if to catch it by surprise. No luck. This time it was the turn of the hairdresser's apprentice, washing the windows of her shop, to look strangely at him. Tim gave up and trudged off to school.

When Mum arrived with Steffy she called him over. 'I forgot to tell you, Tim,' she said. 'Steffy's going to Amanda's after school, so I won't come up for you. Come straight home, won't you?'

Tim's heart leaped at this unexpected second chance. However, the whole school day stretching ahead of him seemed an eternity, even with the Matchbox catalogue to look at during breaks – he'd seen all the stuff by now, anyway. But as it turned out it was a good day. In the morning they had Creative Writing again. Tim was doing the story of the Grand Vizier and the dragons, and Miss Barker had said he could do it in chapters, since it was going to be too long to finish in one day. In the afternoon, Miss Barker read them a very exciting story about a boy and a dog having to rescue the boy's father, who had become trapped on thin ice and was just about to fall through into the freezing water.

Tim decided not to ask for the ice skates.

Chapter 9

Tim raced down the stairs and across the empty playground, his bag bumping on his back. He crossed the road with a few last stragglers from school, and walked quickly down to the shops. Mr Shy's shop was back – in fact, Mr Shy himself was still in the window, fiddling with the ice skates, as he had been the previous day. Tim waved to him and stepped into the dim interior of the shop. He took the shoe-box out and put it on the counter.

'Have fun with them?' enquired Mr Shy, joining him.

'Sort of.' Tim eyed the slippers as Mr Shy drew them out. They were considerably more battered than when he had borrowed them, and one was quite singed and blackened. 'I'm sorry they're a bit messy.'

'Oh, they usually come back like that,' said Mr Shy casually. 'And now what would you like? Some deep-sea diver's boots?'

Tim had visions of sharks, collapsing wrecks, giant clams. 'Look,' he said. 'Some of these shoes are a bit dangerous, aren't they? For little kids?'

Mr Shy spread his hands. 'Well, you can't have adventures without a bit of danger, can you?'

'I don't know . . . I thought if something was magic . . .'

'You thought magic was all silver wands, and fairies on toadstools, didn't you?' Mr Shy wheezed. 'Look in your dictionary, boy. Magic is the stuff that's beyond human power. The forces we don't understand and can't control. Forces, boy. Magic'll make you fly, but you'll fly where it wants you to go.'

'But can't you give me some shoes that are . . . safe?' Tim demanded.

'It's safe you want, is it? Well, you'll be safe enough with this.' Mr Shy produced a box from under the counter and pushed it to Tim.

'Not skates, are they?' asked Tim warily.

Mr Shy laughed and got out his cards. 'Scared of thin ice?'

Tim stared at him, open-mouthed. Mr Shy waved him away impatiently, writing busily with his feather pen in the other hand. 'Off you go, boy. More customers to see to.'

'Where are they?' Tim looked around curiously.

'They won't come till you've gone. Very private library, this. I'll see you tomorrow or the next day. That's if your mother lets you out.' And Mr Shy almost choked himself with wheezing laughter, as though at some private joke.

When Tim got home the back door was open, but the house was quiet. He tiptoed up the stairs and into his mother's room.

'Oh, there you are!' She was lying on the bed, a book open beside her. 'I must have dozed off.'

'Go back to sleep, Mum. I'll play outside.'

'OK,' she smiled, sinking back gratefully. 'There are some biscuits in the jar.'

Tim got himself a drink of apple juice, put two biscuits on a plate and took them out to the little patch of back lawn. The sun was shining through the trees and the bright green grass looked soft and inviting. Tim took a bite of a biscuit, put it back on the plate, then took the shoe-box out of his bag and opened it.

His first reaction was surprise – there was only one shoe. His second thought was one of regret that he couldn't show it to Steffy. She would love

it. The shoe was an old-fashioned buttoned boot, big enough for an adult, made of bright yellow leather with red heel and toe pieces and shiny red buttons. But the thing you noticed even before that was that it had been converted into a little house. It had windows on three or four different levels, including an attic in the little pitched roof that had been added to the top. There were window-boxes in which tiny flowers seemed to be really growing, and checked curtains fluttering. At ground level was a blue-painted door with miniature brass hinges and door-knob.

Tim put the shoe down on the grass and gazed at it. He tried to look in at the windows, but the curtains were all drawn. With a finger and thumb he managed to grasp the little door-knob, but although it turned in his hand the door refused to open. There seemed to be no way of seeing what, if anything, was inside the shoe-house. He took another bite of his biscuit and sat looking at the shoe, conscious of a feeling of disappointment. It was a lovely thing, but there wasn't much you could do with it, except admire it. This must be what Mr Shy meant by something safe. It was as safe as his old teddy-bear upstairs, or Steffy's toy bus. The trouble was, he had come to expect all Mr Shy's shoes to be magic.

The shoe sat quietly on the grass, its secrets locked inside it. Tim looked thoughtfully at it. If it was like the other shoes, the thing to do was to put it on. He inspected the buttons, and tried to undo one. It seemed to be stuck. How do you put on a boot? he wondered. From the top, of course. He stood up and tried the roof. It opened wide on a little hinge, and without pausing to look inside, Tim poked his toe in and pushed.

Tim landed on a bed and bounced on to the floor. Looking up, he saw the blue sky disappear as the roof swung back into its normal position. He got up and looked around. On one of the other beds a boy was sitting. He stared at Tim.

'Gor blimey, I'm hungry!' he announced.

Tim looked back at his new friend. The boy was about his age and height, but very thin, almost a skeleton, with dark eyes in a white face and ragged clothes hanging off his body.

'What's your name?' Tim enquired.

'What's the matter with you?' retorted the boy. 'Did you hit your head on the ceiling?'

'I might have.' Tim looked down at himself. He, too was dressed in rags. Just then there were shouts outside the door, and some sounds of scuffling, followed by a series of thumps. The other boy took no notice.

There was a moment's pause, then the door burst open and five or six children of assorted sizes burst into the room, tumbling over each other and shouting at the tops of their voices. They had an old rag doll, which they tossed from one to the other as they raced around the room, jumping on the beds and knocking things over. A small girl appeared in the doorway, jumping up and down.

'Nick! Nick!' she shrilled. 'They've got my dolly!'

Tim's companion, to whom this remark appeared to be addressed, still took no notice. The older children shrieked with laughter as they took turns to dangle the doll in front of the little girl and then, as she grabbed at it, throw it high in the air out of her reach. The little girl screamed and slapped at them, occasionally crying, 'Help me, Nick!'

Before long Tim could not stand it. He grabbed the doll in mid-flight and, before the others had realized what he was doing, had handed it to the little girl. She smiled at him. Tears had made long streaks down her grubby cheeks, and her yellow hair was matted, but there was something about her that reminded Tim of Steffy.

The older children now turned their attention to Tim. Two or three of the boys rushed at him. He pushed one of them in the chest, sending him off-balance, and backed away. He felt the wall behind him as the others advanced on him.

Just then a bigger girl put her head around the door. 'She's coming!' she hissed. Instantly there was a rush for the door, the children clawing at each other in the scramble to get out. Within a few seconds the room was empty except for Tim, Nick and two other boys, who threw themselves down on the remaining beds and lay quietly. There was a breathless pause, and then a bulky shape loomed in the doorway.

'What's going on here?' enquired a harsh voice.

At first Tim thought she was a witch. She was a big old woman, as broad as she was tall, with a long thin nose meandering down her face and coarse grey hair straggling out of a big green-spotted head-scarf. She was wearing a large, grubby apron over voluminous dark-blue skirts, and she leaned in the doorway, panting.

'You'll be the death of me, you kids,' she complained. 'Up and down them stairs. What have I done, to get visited with so many of yer?' She glared at Tim. 'Look at this mess!' she scolded. 'Clean it up, or there'll be no supper for you!'

Tim opened his mouth to protest, but she had gone. The other boys sniggered. Tim looked at the jumble of clothes, blankets and broken toys on the floor, and he looked at the other boys. 'Well, I'm not going to clean it up,' he announced.

'You have to,' said one of the others. He dragged a torn scrap of a comic out of his pocket and buried his nose in it.

'I didn't make the mess,' pursued Tim.

'So what?' said the other boy, edging round to where he could peer at the comic over the first boy's shoulder. 'She doesn't care.'

'Well, it's not fair,' said Tim firmly.

'Aw, you'd better clean it up,' said Nick, a note of anxiety in his voice. 'You won't get any supper.'

'I mightn't want any.'

'Not want any supper?' Nick sounded incredulous. Tim thought about it. He was rather hungry. He remembered with regret the biscuits he had left outside on the grass. He went to the window and looked out, wondering if he'd see them there, and what size they would be. But all he could see was grass, normal-size, and trees in the distance.

'Well,' he said, turning back to the room. 'Who's going to help me?'

This question was received in stony silence. Reluctantly, Tim started to wander around the room, picking up things and putting them away as best he could. After a few minutes he became aware that someone was behind him. Looking round, he saw that the little girl had crept back into the room and was quietly straightening up the beds. She gave him a timid smile.

'Thanks,' said Tim, smiling back.

'Gertie, Gertie, always dirty,' chanted one of the other boys softly, but when Tim glared at him he stopped.

Tim and Gertie worked in silence. After a while Nick looked up as Tim was shoving a bundle of clothes into a cupboard. 'They don't go there,' he said gruffly. 'Look, I'll show you.' He opened some drawers and began to pack the clothes away.

With Nick's help they soon had the room reasonably tidy. Tim threw himself down on his bed, tired after this effort, but almost immediately a bell started ringing somewhere downstairs. The other boys leaped up and charged for the doorway, fighting each other to be the first out. Gertie scratched about, trying to squeeze between their legs as they struggled to get through the door.

'What is it?' asked Tim in alarm, looking about for a fire.

'Supper!' cried Nick. 'Aren't you starving?'

By now, Tim really was hungry. He joined the throng of children streaming down the stairs. They were jostling and bumping each other, and he took Gertie's hand protectively. Soon they arrived in a large, bare room, with a grimy wooden table down the middle. At the head of the table stood the old woman, very red in the face, and with fresh stains down the front of her apron. She had a

big soup ladle in her hand, and was doling something from a big steaming pot into chipped enamel bowls, and handing them out to the children who were lined up to one side of her.

'Don't push! Don't shove! Stop yer noise!' she screeched constantly at them. The children close to her were quiet enough, but those at a safer distance were surreptitiously elbowing each other and treading on each other's toes. As each child was served, he or she went to sit on a stool at the table, and there were slurping sounds as they hastily shovelled the soup into their mouths.

At last Tim's turn came. He looked with dismay at the thin, greyish liquid in the pot, with transparent globules of fat floating around on it. The old woman glared at him.

'Did you tidy that room?' she demanded.

'Yes.'

'Here's your supper, then.' She slopped in a small helping of the broth. Tim looked at it.

'Is that all I get?' he ventured.

'WHAT?'

'Could I have some bread?'

The old woman drew herself up to her full height. Her eyes glittered terribly.

'What's this boy's name?' she bellowed.

'Theodore!' screamed the other children in gleeful chorus. Tim winced. How he hated that name.

'Well, Theodore,' snarled the old woman. 'Never before has a boy asked for bread. You're first in line for spanking tonight.' And she turned to the next child, who was waiting eagerly for her broth.

Furious, Tim trudged to the table and sat down in an empty place. Gertie squeezed his arm, and even Nick was looking sympathetic. 'I'll show her,' Tim thought to himself. 'I've killed three dragons. She can't treat me like this.'

But it was one thing to plot revenge, and another to work out exactly how to carry it out; and after supper, when the children lined up again, Tim found himself pushed to the front, where he was roughly bent over the old woman's knee and walloped hard three or four times.

'Oh, how it hurts me hand!' the old woman complained. 'And so many of yer in the line!'

That night, Tim sat gloomily on his bed in the attic room. Several of the children had gathered there, because it wasn't as dark as the other bedrooms, with light from the waning moon streaming in through the window. Nick and some of the others were playing knuckle-bones on the floor, some girls were playing noughts and crosses on a scrap of paper, and Gertie was gazing out the window, whispering occasionally to her rag doll. It had been explained to Tim that bedtime always followed suppertime, but it was much too early to go to sleep, and the old woman was too lazy to climb the stairs more than once or twice a day to see what they were doing. A guard was posted at the door, just in case.

'It's not right,' said Tim at last. 'I don't know why you put up with it, the way she treats you.'

'What else can we do?' shrugged Nick.

'You could run away.'

'Where to?' sneered another boy.

'Besides,' said a third boy, 'we can't get out.'

'Well, what about when you go outside to play? She can't watch all of you, all the time.'

'That's why she never lets us go outside,' explained Nick.

'What, never?'

'Never.'

Tim looked around. Certainly, all the children had unnaturally pale skin. His mother always said he didn't tan, but compared to these children he was dark brown.

'Why don't you sneak out, when she's not looking?' he demanded.

'She's always looking,' said a tall red-haired girl. 'And she keeps the door locked all the time.'

Tim went over to the window where Gertie was. It was firmly nailed in place, and there didn't seem to be any part of it that opened. He wondered about breaking the glass, but the panes were so small, with solid timber between them, that there would still not be enough room to climb out. He tried hard to remember what the shoe-house had looked like from the outside. It seemed to him that all the windows were the same sort.

'Well, she's not going to keep me locked up here,' he said. 'I'll find a way to escape. I've killed three dragons,' he added proudly.

The others showed no sign of being impressed by this information.

'Yep,' said Tim. 'Three of 'em.'

'Is that so?' said Nick casually. 'We had a girl here who said she'd killed a shark, and escaped from a giant clam.'

'Really?' Tim wondered if this was another of Mr Shy's customers. 'Where is she now?'

'Dunno. She disappeared. Maybe she got away.'

Tim was encouraged by this. He sat down again on his bed, wrapped in thought. 'She must have a key,' he muttered, thinking aloud. 'She must go out some time.'

'She keeps it in her apron pocket,' contributed Nick.

'What about when she goes to bed?'

'She puts it under her pillow,' said Gertie, turning from the window. The others looked at her in astonishment.

'How do you know?'

'We watched her, me and dolly. Through a crack in the door.'

'Well, that settles it,' announced Tim. 'I'm getting out tonight, as soon as she's asleep. Who's coming with me?'

To his surprise, no-one answered. Instead, the children seemed to melt away. One minute the room was full, the next minute they had all crept away, presumably to their own rooms. The two boys who shared the attic room with Tim and Nick had slipped into their own beds and pulled the covers over their heads. Only Nick and Gertie remained where they were.

'What's wrong with everyone?' asked Tim.

Nick shrugged. 'They're scared.'

'Don't they want to go home?'

Nick looked blank. 'Home?'

Tim was perplexed. 'Well, she's not your mother, surely? Or the mother of any of the other kids? Haven't you all got real mothers and families somewhere outside?'

Nick frowned. 'I don't know. I . . . don't remember being anywhere else.'

'What about you, Gertie?'

'I don't know.' Gertie screwed up her face, concentrating. 'Maybe . . . I think dolly can remember something.' She stared into the blank face of her rag doll.

'Well, come out with me anyway,' said Tim. 'I've got a home. You can both come there, and my Mum'll look after you.'

'I'm coming,' said Gertie firmly.

'I . . . I'll help you,' said Nick, but he looked worried.

They waited. The moon slowly moved higher in the sky, then started to slip downwards. Occasionally there were noises downstairs, doors opening and closing, footsteps. Then for a long time there was silence. At last Tim said, 'I think it's time.'

Gertie was dozing. They gently shook her awake, then the three of them tiptoed to the door. Suddenly Gertie gave a little squeal and rushed back into the

94

room. She re-emerged a few seconds later clutching her doll. Tim had brought one of the blankets off his bed. Nick looked at it enquiringly. Tim shrugged. He did not feel capable of explaining that blankets were the only weapons he knew how to use.

They crept down the stairs, stopping occasionally to listen. The only sounds were sleep sounds – breathing, an occasional cough, the groan of bedsprings as someone turned over. Sometimes a stair creaked, and Tim held his breath.

The old woman slept downstairs in the toe of the shoe, next to the front door. Even with her bedroom door shut they could hear her snoring. Tim turned the handle very, very slowly. There was a faint click as the latch opened. They all froze. The old woman grunted, turned over in bed and settled back into her deep sleep. There was an empty bottle lying on the floor beside her, and the smell of her breath reminded Tim of an old man who had once staggered up to him in the street and asked for a dollar for the bus fare home.

Tim started to tiptoe towards the old woman's bed, but Gertie took his arm, shaking her head. He stopped, and she slipped past him, skittering across the floor on her hands and knees. She was so small and light she made no more noise than a cat. Tim and Nick watched, their nerves tingling, and she slipped her hand under the pillow and groped around for what seemed like ages. At last she turned to them, triumphantly holding up something that flashed in the moonlight. Then she crawled back again, the key between her teeth.

They gathered around the front door. Tim handed his blanket to Nick and slipped the key into the lock. It was difficult to get it right in – it seemed stiff and clumsy. At last he managed it, but not before the key had produced a loud grating sound. Gertie jumped up and down in her agitation and Nick retreated to the foot of the stairs, his eyes bulging.

Tim tried the key. It wouldn't turn the first way he tried. There was a gasp from Gertie and he looked up to see the old woman in the doorway of her room, rubbing her eyes. Nick seemed to have frozen on the stairs. Desperately, Tim turned the key the other way. There was a click. The old woman began to bellow as Tim struggled to pull the heavy door open. Everything seemed to be happening in slow motion. Tim grabbed Gertie and bundled her out the door.

'The blanket!' he screamed to Nick. Nick seemed to come awake, stared at the blanket in his hands, then threw it right over the old woman's head. She blundered about, roaring and reaching out to grab Tim. He skipped out of the way. 'Come on!' he yelled to Nick. 'Quick!'

But Nick, his eyes wide with terror, shook his head several times, then turned and bolted up the stairs. The old woman was clutching at the blanket, and had managed to find the door with her other hand. Tim raced around her and dived through the narrowing gap as she pushed it shut. He landed on the grass, the sound of the door slamming ringing in his ears.

After a while Tim sat up and looked around. He

was on his own back lawn, and the shoe-house was back in its box beside him. There was no sign of Gertie, but he could hear his mother's voice, from inside the house, calling him.

Quickly Tim pushed the shoe-box back into his school bag. Then he grabbed the biscuits, which still lay on their plate on the grass, and crammed them both into his mouth. He was starving.

His mother came out, looking relaxed and happy. 'It's time to go and fetch Steffy,' she said. 'Do you want to come?'

Chapter 10

Tim's mother watched him as she doled cabbage and stew on to his plate. They were among his least favourite foods, and he had often got himself into trouble in the past by complaining loudly when they appeared on the table.

'Thank you, Mum,' said Tim, picking up his knife and fork and tucking into the food with gusto. She looked at him in amazement.

'Do you like cabbage now?' she enquired.

'No, but it's better than nothing, isn't it?'

Steffy ate voraciously. She liked everything. Between mouthfuls she chattered on about her coming birthday, listing the friends she was going to invite to her party, the presents she hoped to get, the clothes she was going to wear.

Tim sat very quietly. The kitten had managed to scramble into his lap and was curled up there, purring. Watching Steffy eat, he thought how skinny little Gertie would appreciate a meal like this, and he wondered again what had happened to her. It was possible that the old woman had caught her, but somehow he didn't think so. Maybe she had found her way home.

He didn't like to think about Nick. At least the old woman hadn't seen him, and probably didn't even know that someone had helped Tim and Gertie; so Nick would not have got into trouble. Tim thought, with a shudder, of venturing into the shoe-house again, and trying to persuade Nick to escape with him; but he wasn't at all sure he could do it, and the chances of getting out a second time himself seemed slim.

The next morning he got up extra early and cooked breakfast. He made boiled eggs – two for himself, because he was still feeling unusually hungry. Mum was able to read the paper while they had breakfast, something she rarely had time to do.

'Oh, look!' she exclaimed. 'They found that little girl!'

Tim pricked up his ears. 'What little girl?'

'This little girl who went missing about a year ago. There was a big search, but . . . Listen: "Trudi Petersen was four years old when she disappeared from her parents' home in . . . hmmm . . . Trudi was found last night wandering in a park less than a kilometre from her home. She was unable to tell police where she had been for the past year. Trudi was emaciated but unharmed . . ." '

'What does emac . . . that word mean?'

'Oh . . . very thin. She hadn't been getting enough to eat. It goes on: "Trudi was still clutching her favourite rag doll, which had been in her possession at the time of the supposed abduction." Oh dear. You children really must be careful.'

There was a picture in the newspaper, but it was so blurred Tim could not make out the little girl's features.

'What sort of name is Trudi?' he asked. 'Is it short for anything?'

'It used to be short for Gertrude, but that's a rather old-fashioned name.'

Mr Shy was not there when they passed that morning on their way to school, and in the afternoon Tim was invited to Phillip's house, and Mum picked him up in the car. He worried a bit about whether Mr Shy had been expecting him, but on the whole he felt that he was keeping to the rules. He was supposed to go into the shop if it was there when he passed – so if he didn't happen to go that way there was nothing he could do about it.

Nothing happened the next day, either, except the weekly phone call. Tim got out the world globe and traced the route from Sydney to Ottawa while he was waiting for his turn to speak. It was hard to believe that you could talk to someone who was so far away. No wonder it cost so much. Tim wished his mother didn't worry so much about money. There were times when he would have given anything to pick up the phone and ring his father, to tell him everything, big things like Mr Shy, and little things like Ricky always snatching his pencil in class and getting him into trouble. You couldn't say anything much when you got one minute, once a week.

Tim's father sounded cheerful, as usual. Undeterred by the threat of thin ice, he had been learning to skate on a canal. When he got home he would take Tim and Steffy to an ice rink and they would all learn.

100

'I can't wait!' cried Steffy, jumping up and down, when she heard this. Tim thought that you'd probably be safe enough at an ice rink, but he was still glad he hadn't borrowed Mr Shy's skates.

As it happened it was almost a week before Mr Shy popped up again. It made Tim a little uncomfortable to have the shoe-house in his school bag all that time. A couple of times he took it out, when no-one was around, and looked at it. Once more the curtains were tightly shut, and he could not see inside. He put his ear close to it and listened. You might expect to hear those children shouting and thumping – they were the noisiest bunch Tim had ever met, even worse than Miss Moodie's class, who could be heard all over the school sometimes. However, no sounds came from the shoe-house. It was very light, too – it was hard to believe there was anything at all inside it. Tim thought of shaking it to see if it rattled, but decided against it.

The days dragged on. On Thursday they had Special Assembly. Tim quite liked sitting in the school hall and singing songs, and occasionally there would be a special item. Phillip had played the piano a couple of times, to thunderous applause from his classmates. But then came the presentations, which Tim hated, when Kylie and her friends always got Merit Certificates. Tim had only ever got one, for Trying Hard in Craft; and that was only because they tried to be fair and give them to everybody. Steffy had got one already this year, for Cleaning the Blackboard, or some such thing.

Tim gritted his teeth when they came to his class. Sure enough, Kylie's name was read out first: a Merit Certificate for Consistent Work in Spelling. Next was a pleasant surprise: Phillip, for Great Improvement in Maths. Tim clapped loudly and kept clapping when everyone else had finished, so he didn't hear his name read out, and the school captain had to read it again: 'Tim Morrison, for Writing Fantastic Stories'. Tim had felt slightly guilty when Miss Barker praised his story about the dragons for being 'imaginative', but he did feel he deserved some credit for writing four whole pages. He stumbled out to the front in a daze, then a big grin spread over his face, and he couldn't stop grinning, he felt, for hours.

That afternoon Mum and Steffy went off to buy party hats and balloons. Tim found himself walking through the shopping centre by himself, and at long last there was Mr Shy.

Tim looked quickly over his shoulder to make sure no-one was watching, then slipped into the shop. Mr Shy was sewing again. He had nearly finished a little jacket, which he shoved under the counter when he saw Tim.

'Is that for an elf?' Tim couldn't help asking.

'Thought you didn't believe in elves, and suchlike,' replied Mr Shy, adjusting his glasses to peer up at Tim.

'I didn't say that.' Tim put the shoe-box on the counter.

'Let you out, did she?' wheezed Mr Shy.

'Very funny. I thought you said there wouldn't be any trouble with this one.'

'You should learn to listen, boy. I said you'd be safe.'

'And anyway,' went on Tim. 'What's going to happen to the other children in there?'

Mr Shy shrugged.

'I nearly didn't get out myself,' persisted Tim. 'I reckon you tricked me into going in there. I reckon that was a rotten thing to do.'

He stopped, wondering if he'd gone too far. It wasn't the way you were supposed to talk to adults. Mr Shy looked at Tim through first one pair of glasses, then the other. Then, apparently not satisfied with the view he was getting, he took off both pairs of glasses and peered at Tim without them.

'I don't think Gertrude's parents would agree with you,' he said at last.

Tim was silenced for a bit, then he said, 'Could I look around for a while?'

'Certainly. Browsing is encouraged between the hours of three and four.'

Tim wandered around, picking up boxes from the shelves, examining their contents, then carefully putting them back where he had found them. There were shoes and sandals and slippers and boots of every description: snowshoes, flippers, wooden clogs, high-heeled boots with wicked-looking spurs attached, mocassins, Roman sandals, ballet shoes. An idea struck Tim.

'Could I borrow for someone else?' he asked.

'Who?'

'Well, it's my little sister's birthday tomorrow, and I wondered . . .'

'She can join the library herself. Bring her in one day.'

'I don't think so,' said Tim doubtfully. 'She's not very good with secrets, and . . . couldn't I just borrow something for her this once?'

'All right, but I'll have to do her a card.' And Mr Shy armed himself with pen, ink and cards. 'How do you spell her name?'

'S-T-E-P-H-A-N-I-E.' Tim was looking through boxes as he talked, quite taken with his new idea. 'She'd love these!' He picked up some glittering red shoes that caught the light and flashed fire.

Mr Shy looked up sharply: 'Put those back!'

'What wrong? Are they the witch's shoes from *The Wizard of Oz*?'

'No, boy. There's worse in the world than that.'

Tim quickly put the red shoes back in their box. There was something creepy about them, and he seemed to remember that there was a scary story about some red shoes; but he couldn't remember what happened.

The next box yielded an exquisite pair of glass slippers. 'Oh, look at these!'

'A much better choice,' beamed Mr Shy. Tim put them in his bag.

'And what about yourself?'

'Oh, can I still borrow some?' Tim looked around. 'But . . . what's the time?' Now that he thought about it, he must have been in the shop for ages.

'Late. Very, very late,' said Mr Shy mournfully. Tim darted back to the counter and grabbed his school bag.

'Sorry, Mr Shy – I've got to go,' he said. Mr Shy thrust a large parcel at him.

'This is what you want. Put 'em on as soon as you get outside.'

Tim was in too much of a hurry to worry about being suspicious. He rushed out of the shop and tore open the parcel. To his delight, he found the boots that had adorned Mr Shy's window the first time he had ever seen it. He put his own shoes in his bag and pulled on the boots.

Nothing happened. Tim looked down at his feet. The boots were firmly on. He looked back at the shop. Mr Shy had come to the door and was polishing the brass door-knob.

'What are these?' Tim called back to him.

'Seven-league boots,' called back Mr Shy. 'Better hurry home, boy. Your mother's nearly there.'

Wasting no more time on questions, Tim set off at a run. At least, he took one running step . . . but when his foot hit the ground he found to his astonishment that he was outside his own house. He took another step, and this time he felt himself spring into the air and come down immediately in the park on the other side of the main road. Quickly he turned and took a step back the way he had come, landing on his own doorstep again. This time Tim sat down and pulled off the boots. Then he found the key in his pocket, unlocked the door and slipped inside. He had barely shoved the boots in his school bag and thrown himself down on a chair when he heard Steffy's excited voice outside and she burst in, followed by their mother, and spilling parcels and paper bags all over the kitchen table.

At dinnertime, their mother didn't eat anything. Instead, she said, 'I'm going out tonight.'

'Who's going to baby-sit us?' demanded Steffy.

'Karen's coming.'

'What about my birthday cake? When are you going to make that?'

'It's all right, Steffy. It's all been done. I'm going to have a well-earned night out, having dinner with the Harrises. I might be late, so don't wake me until eight o'clock in the morning.'

Tim was delighted. As soon as he got an opportunity he whispered to Steffy: 'If you do exactly what I say tonight, you'll get a nice surprise.'

'What? What is it?'

'Shhh.' Tim put his finger to his lips. 'If you say anything . . . no surprise.'

Steffy looked a bit suspicious, but she kept quiet.

When their mother had gone and Karen, the babysitter, was comfortably installed, Tim said, 'Steffy and I are tired. We're going to bed early tonight.' Steffy opened her mouth to object, but Tim nudged her and made terrible faces.

'Oh, good,' Karen was saying. 'There's a great movie on Channel Ten. It's not recommended for children.'

Karen was fat, and had never been known to climb the stairs to check on the children. Besides, she was addicted to television, and would remain glued to the set all night. She took very little notice as Tim ushered Steffy in and out of the bathroom. When they looked into the living room to say goodnight she gave them a little wave, her eyes never leaving the screen.

Tim refused to say anything to Steffy until they were safely inside their room, then he drew the shoe-box out of its hiding-place and handed it to her, saying, 'Happy Birthday'.

Steffy pulled out the shoes and put them on the rug in front of her. 'Feel them, Tim,' she said softly. Tim touched one. It was smooth and cool.

'Cinderella's glass slippers,' murmured Steffy, holding one up so that it caught the light and flashed dazzling colours around the room.

'Listen, Steffy,' said Tim. 'It's only for a lend, but . . . they're magic slippers. If you put them on, you'll . . . sort of . . . be Cinderella.'

'Will I get a beautiful dress?'

'I suppose so.'

'And go to the ball?'

'Probably . . . I don't know exactly what will happen. You just have to try it and see.'

'Wait a minute,' said Steffy. 'We have to get ready.' To Tim's surprise she darted out of the room. A few minutes later she was back, holding a large pineapple.

'What's that for?'

'There aren't any pumpkins in the kitchen. Do you think this will do? For my carriage?'

'I suppose so. What about the horses?'

'That's easy. I'll have just one horse.' Steffy rummaged in her underwear drawer and came up with the sleeping kitten.

'How did he get there?' asked Tim in surprise.

'That's his bed now,' said Steffy. 'I said he could

107

have it. Now, I need some footmen.'

'We haven't got any mice,' said Tim positively.

'I know!' Steffy rushed out of the room again.

'Quiet!' Tim hissed after her. 'Don't let Karen hear!'

A few minutes later Steffy was back, cupping something carefully in her hands. 'Come on, darlings,' she whispered. 'You're going to have an adventure.'

'What have you got?' Tim came closer to look. 'Oh, yuk, Steffy!'

Crawling around in her hands were two enormous black cockroaches.

'They're my friends!' Steffy was never frightened of creepy crawly things. 'Now, we're all set.'

She arranged the pineapple with the kitten standing in front of it and the cockroaches crawling around on top. After a few false starts, with the kitten wandering off, and on one occasion trying to hunt the cockroaches, she managed to get them

more or less into the proper order and at the same time to pull on the slippers.

There was a blinding flash. When Tim could see again, Steffy had gone. Tim's heart sank as he realized he had forgotten to tell Steffy about taking off the shoes. Maybe she had been whisked away to some strange land from which she would never return. What would he tell Mum? Was this how Gertie's family had felt?

Just then he heard a pattering sound at the window. He raced over and looked out.

Steffy was standing below, about to let fly with another handful of small stones. When she saw Tim, she called softly, 'Look at me!'

Tim looked and looked. She was wearing a long cloudy dress that might have been pale blue and might have been silver, with glittering things here and there on it. Her hair was fastened up with something glittering too, and her cheeks were flushed with excitement. Behind her, on the cobbled lane at the side of the house, stood a pretty little golden coach, attended by two men in shiny black livery – Tim disliked their beetle-browed looks immediately – and hitched up to a most unusual grey and black striped horse, which twitched its tail and looked cross.

'Fantastic!' said Tim. 'Now listen, Steffy. If you get into any trouble, take the shoes off, OK?'

'OK. And I have to be back by midnight, right?'

'Yes, and make sure you are. Otherwise you might lose one of the shoes, and I'll get into trouble with Mr Shy.'

'Who's Mr Shy?'

'Never mind. Off you go. Have a good time at the ball.'

Steffy stepped daintily into the carriage, turning to wave to Tim. He waved back, and kept waving as the little equipage clip-clopped down the lane and disappeared round the corner.

Chapter 11

Tim found some cushions and arranged them in Steffy's bed so that they looked roughly like a sleeping child – just in case Karen should climb the stairs for the first time ever. Then he turned off the light and got into his own bed. He supposed Steffy would wake him when she came in at midnight – meanwhile he ought to get some sleep.

But Tim could not sleep. He lay very still and tried to turn the thoughts crowding through his mind into dreams, but it didn't work. His brain was racing with excitement and he couldn't work out how to slow it down. Besides, there were the seven-league boots, which he'd hardly had on his feet . . .

Tim got out of bed and took the boots out of their hiding-place in the dress-ups box. They posed rather a problem, being too big to fit into his school bag. He wasn't sure how he was going to get them back to Mr Shy without being noticed.

He stroked the supple leather, then went to the window, still holding the boots, and looked out. Between the roof-tops he could see the twinkling lights of the city. He wondered where Steffy and her carriage were. He looked back at his bed. It didn't look at all inviting. Quickly, Tim scooped up the rest of the cushions from the floor and stuffed them under the covers of his bed. He went over to the door and looked back. Both beds looked quite convincing. Finally, Tim went back to the window and drew on the boots.

His first cautious step through the window took Tim on to the roof of his school, where he landed precariously on the mossy slates. He grabbed a chimney to keep himself from slipping off the steep roof, and gazed down at the ships lying by the container wharf, so brightly lit it could have been day. Another step took him to the top of a tall city building. The parapet where he landed was in darkness, but the buildings around him were lit up and coloured signs flashed constantly around him. Below, on the roof of another building, was a floodlit swimming pool. Someone was swimming slowly up and down, and other people were lounging by the edge, sipping drinks. Tim took another, bigger step and found himself on a windswept cliff. The city was far beneath him, and he was looking out to sea.

Taking a deep breath, he strode out again. In mid-air he had a panicky feeling that he'd just done something really stupid – because where could he land in the Pacific Ocean? He took a few more steps in mid-air, and found to his surprise that they enabled him to go further. This time, he came down on the deck of a big ship. A man standing nearby with a glass in his hand stared at Tim, shook his head and stared again, then looked at the glass in his hand and tipped the contents over the rail into the water. Then he staggered away. Tim stayed on the ship for a few minutes, enjoying the gentle roll of the ocean beneath him. There were lights on the ship, but they were dim, and there was no-one else around. The sea was very dark.

Tim stepped out once more. A few mid-air steps took him to a beach with warm white sand and swaying palm-trees. Out to sea, the sky was streaked with pink. Tim was puzzled at first, because he knew he had not been travelling for long; but then he remembered the time difference in different parts of the world.

A tremendous idea seized him. He remembered the globe of the world, and how he had traced the route to Canada. He closed his eyes and concentrated on remembering the outlines of countries, the bumps of mountains; then he strode out again, this time veering to the left of the rising sun. A few frantic steps in mid-air, and he found himself standing on hard-packed snow high up on a craggy mountain. The air was thin and cold, and Tim shivered in his light-weight pyjamas. Another step took him high over a wide land which stretched below him, with mountains and valleys, pale sparkling lakes and endless pine forests, great flat plains covered with snow, and city after city all bathed in feeble early-morning winter sunshine.

He landed on a slope above a city. He saw roads cut through huge banks of snow which formed high walls on either side. There were cars abandoned, buried in snow so that only their roofs showed. Some children, laughing and shrieking, had built a

snowman. A door opened in a nearby house, a voice called to them, and they raced towards it, pushing each other, their voices carrying through the clear air. A few people walking briskly along the paths of the city were well wrapped-up with hats, scarves and fur-lined boots. There was a sort of frozen river with very straight sides, crossed by a few bridges, and people were skating. Tim could see a tall man wobbling along, supported on either side by a laughing teenage boy and girl. There was something familiar about his red and yellow

striped scarf. Tim had seen his mother knitting
one just like it . . .

'Dad!' he whispered.

The man slipped and nearly fell to the ice. The
girl grabbed his arm. Tim could hear their peals of
laughter. One step and he could be with them. He
could already hear his father's shout of recogni-
tion as he scooped Tim up into his arms. He could
smell the warm smell of his father, and feel the
scratchy wool of his father's jacket against his
cheek. But what then? How could Tim possibly

115

explain how he had got there? Maybe people would think his father had gone mad, and lock him up.

With a last longing look at the people on the ice, Tim turned away and pressed on. The cold was beginning to make him very uncomfortable, so he veered towards what he hoped was the south. His first step took him to a point high over another city. This one, with its cluster of incredibly tall buildings, was easy to recognize, especially when he looked around and found that he was standing on the head of the Statue of Liberty. Her torch soared above him, higher than the steeple on the church near his school.

A huge step, and several more in the air, took Tim over another ocean, this one sparkling in sunshine and busy with ships steaming in all directions. He kept veering to the right, and was rewarded with a rush of warm air on his next landing. He looked around and found himself in a barren place, with dry, stony ground, a few low buildings the same colour as the ground, and nothing else under a deep blue sky. Tim took off again, to find himself in a steamy jungle clearing, where a profusion of creepers, some with brightly-coloured flowers, seemed to smother the tall trees, and the air was full of the cries of birds and other strange creatures. Tim felt a prickling at the back of his neck. Whipping around, he saw a yellow-eyed tiger, its belly flat to the ground, stalking him. As it sprang so did he, soaring over the tree-tops to another desert, where he landed on the top of a vast, crumbling pyramid. Two more steps took

116

him to a hot, teeming city, with narrow streets winding between tumble-down stone buildings, and dark-eyed people who plucked at his sleeves, holding out cupped hands; then on to another mountain-top, so high he felt dizzy, and could hardly breathe. Looking down one of its icy slopes he saw two enormous, ape-like creatures shambling off in hasty retreat. One was twice as tall as a human, and had flowing reddish hair over its entire body. The other was stooped, making it appear smaller, and its hair was silvery. Tim felt sorry to have frightened them away. He leaped from the mountain-top, to find himself in a strange settlement of flimsy wooden houses which stood on stilts in a steamy swamp. The dark-skinned people were wrapped in brilliantly-coloured cloth, and they smiled in welcome and spoke to him in a strange language. Tim hurried on. The sun was sinking and the sky was turning a deep orange when he landed on hard red earth in the middle of a flock of emus, which thundered away into a cloud of dust. Tim smiled and took off again.

It was pitch-dark now, and Tim took several mid-air steps in what he hoped was the right direction. He landed in a paddock that looked familiar. A tiny step took him up to a window and he peered in. There was his cousin Jason, sitting up in bed, reading a Tintin book. Tim imagined the look on Jason's face if he should tap on the glass, pull a face at him and then disappear. The very thought gave him a fit of the giggles, but he resisted the temptation. Landing here had given

117

him his bearings, however, and after a moment's thought he stepped out confidently. By a miracle of navigation, or perhaps because the boots had a built-in ability to find their way home, he landed this time right on his own windowsill. He was about to step inside when he thought better of it. In these boots, even a tiny step might take him through the room, down the stairs and into Karen's lap. Instead, he carefully took off the boots, clambered down from the windowsill, and threw himself down on his bed. No wonder, he thought sleepily, his father was always tired after those long trips around the world . . .

Tim awoke with a start, what seemed a few seconds later, to find Steffy bending over him. She was holding the struggling kitten under one arm.

'Let him go,' mumbled Tim, still half asleep. 'He'll scratch you.'

'He's been a very naughty kitty,' said Steffy, letting the kitten go. He burrowed into Tim's bed, and a few moments later his muffled purring could be heard from around Tim's feet. Tim sat up and turned his reading light on. Steffy was back in her pyjamas, her cheeks very pink and her eyes bright.

'How did it go?' demanded Tim.

'It was great!' Steffy got up and danced around the room. 'There weren't any lights, Tim, like you switch on, but thousands and thousands and thousands of candles, all hanging in clusters, and the roof was one big mirror, so you could see everything, all shiny . . .'

'What else?'

'Oh, ladies in lovely dresses, and . . . I thought I'd be the only little girl, but there were lots of children, all sizes, but of course I was the beautifullest, and even the Prince said—'

'Wait a minute, Steffy. Begin at the beginning. What was it like in the carriage?'

'Oh Tim, it was weird. As soon as we turned the corner out of the lane, we weren't in our street at all, but some other place, with funny winding streets and little houses with lace curtains and flower-boxes – and I saw a man going round lighting the street-lamps with . . . like . . . a big match. And we rattled along until we got to this palace . . . Except that on the way we saw a mouse, and that naughty horse tried to chase it, and the coachman had to really pull the reins hard. And when we got there the footman got down to tie up the horse and the horse tried to chase him, and he was scuttling away and trying to squeeze under the door into the palace, Tim, and I really had to shout at them all to make them behave. And then later the two of them, coachman and footman, got inside and I found them in the supper-room *on the table* gobbling up all the food, and I had a good mind to bring in the horse and let him at them—'

'You're telling it all mixed-up, Steffy. What happened when you arrived?'

'Well, I went straight in, and they all looked at me, and whispered things like "Who's that?", but that was all right, and then the Prince came over, and he was at *least* ten, and he looked just like Toby in Year Six, and he asked me to dance. I got a fright, Tim, because I suddenly remembered

119

that I didn't know how to dance, but as soon as the music started my feet just knew what to do. And we danced and danced, and had supper – there was lemonade, Tim, and lots of strawberry sponge cakes, except for what my footmen ate – and the Prince said when we're grown up he wants to marry me.' Steffy sighed and danced around the room again with her eyes shut, until she bumped into the chest of drawers and started wailing.

'Shhh!' hissed Tim. 'And what about midnight? What happened?'

'Well!' said Steffy, when she had recovered. 'I kept trying to remember about leaving before midnight, and I knew I had to, but I still forgot, and suddenly the clock started to strike, and I said to the Prince "Is it eleven o'clock?" and he said "No, twelve," so I just ran, and he ran after me. But it wasn't the last stroke of midnight, Tim. The clock had only just started striking and I would have made it, only that naughty horse had knocked over a bottle of milk on someone's doorstep and he was drinking it, and the footmen had disappeared – I think they went back into the supper-room, because later on when I ran round the corner I went past the window and I could hear ladies screaming and someone saying "There's a cockroach in here!". And I don't care if they never find their way home.'

'But what about the coach?'

'Well, the driver wasn't there, so I jumped in front myself, and grabbed the reins, only of course my shoe fell off and the Prince tried to grab it, but

I got there first, and he was shouting "You have to leave it for me" and I was shouting "No, no, I can't go home without it" and then do you know what, Tim? He pinched me! So then I bit him, and he started crying, and saying "I'm going to tell my Mummy, and she'll have you beheaded", and silly things like that. And then the horse started meowing, and the Prince was saying "Let me have the slipper or I won't marry you," so I said "Who cares?". And I picked up the horse – kitten, I mean – and ran.'

'Did you still have your ball-dress on?'

'No, of course not. As soon as the clock finished striking and the horse turned back into a kitty my dress went too. But the funny thing was, when I got round the corner I realized that I still had one glass slipper on and one in my hand. And also I was a bit worried about getting home, because I didn't know where I was. So I remembered what you said, Tim. I kept hold of the kitten, so he wouldn't get left behind, and with the other hand I took the slipper off. And here I am back in our room. Oh!' Steffy's eyes widened in dismay.

'What's wrong?'

'When I did all that I had to put the first slipper down, the one we were fighting over. I've left it behind after all!'

'Oh well, it can't be helped,' said Tim, after some thought. 'It's part of the story, after all.'

'Anyway, I had a lovely time, Tim,' said Steffy, dancing over to her bed. 'This is the best birthday I've ever had – it is my birthday now, you know, because it's after midnight – and this is the first

121

time I've ever stayed up really late and been to a ball and met a prince and I'm not the least bit tired ...'

And with that Steffy's voice trailed off, and she was asleep. Tim repositioned the kitten so that its head was peeping out from the bedclothes, and settled back to sleep himself.

Chapter 12

Tim woke early, feeling refreshed, but Steffy was still deeply asleep. He seemed to be getting used to night-time adventures, but he guessed she would take a while to recover from hers. Tim went downstairs quietly, fed the kitten and made breakfast for the three of them – meusli and toast. He longed to make a cup of coffee for his mother. He knew exactly what to do, but she still wouldn't let him light the gas without supervision, or handle anything really hot. Instead, he got out the orange juice and some glasses, arranged everything on a tray, and picked it up. After a few adjustments – the tray was too heavy to carry upstairs, so he had to take some of the things separately – he managed to deliver the lot to his mother's bedside. Then he gently woke Steffy and brought her into the room just as the phone rang.

Their father was in high spirits. He talked to Steffy for a long time, since it was her birthday. Then it was Tim's turn.

'Only two more weeks, Tim. Will you be coming to the airport to meet me?'

'You bet.' Tim hesitated. 'Dad, who's teaching you to skate? And do you wear that scarf Mum knitted you?'

'You ask some funny questions, mate. A couple of kids from the next flat are teaching me, Annie and Pierre. I wish you could meet them. And yes, I wear that scarf everywhere. You can't imagine how cold it is here.'

By the time Steffy had opened her presents and exclaimed over them all it was nearly nine. Mum had to drive them to school, and they were still late. Tim had meant to point out that now Steffy was six he was supposed to be taking her to school himself, but it did not seem a good time to mention it.

Steffy yawned a bit throughout the day, and made herself sick eating too much at her party that afternoon, but on the whole she didn't seem badly affected by her late night. One of her presents was a beautifully illustrated book of fairy tales, and she took Tim aside and showed him the Cinderella.

'I was more beautifuller than that, wasn't I, Tim?' she asked.

'Oh yes, Steffy. Much.'

Tim had the glass slipper packed away in his school bag, but there was no sign of Mr Shy that day. The seven-league boots were still in the dress-ups box. Tim hadn't yet worked out what to do about them.

The weekend passed quickly. Various friends and relations came to lunch on the Sunday. Mum insisted that this was not because of Steffy's birthday, and that she was not getting two parties, but a lot of them brought presents for her, and Tim found himself in a rather bad mood for a

124

while. He cheered up when the last arrivals brought a jigsaw puzzle for Steffy and a new Lego book for him, the one with all the stickers.

On Monday morning, Tim prepared his ground carefully. He got up early and persuaded Steffy to get dressed before breakfast. He was too late to actually make breakfast, but he washed the dishes. Then he said, 'Mum, now that Steffy's six, I can take her to school.'

'Well, I don't know . . .'

'Come on, Mum. We've got to start some time.'

'I'll be good,' chimed in Steffy. 'And Tim will look after me.'

'I suppose he will,' conceded their mother. 'You do seem to have grown up a lot in the last few weeks, Tim. Maybe we could give it a try. But if you're late for school, or if you get into any trouble . . .'

'We won't, we won't,' they chorused.

'And you'll have to leave a bit earlier, without me to hurry you along.'

'We're ready now,' said Tim. 'Aren't we, Steffy?'

Steffy ran to get the school bags, and their mother kissed them goodbye at the door.

'We'll be home by half-past three,' Tim promised.

'You make sure you are, or this'll be the last time. And be careful crossing the roads . . .'

At the first corner Tim turned and looked back. Their mother was standing at the gate watching them. He waved.

Steffy talked continuously, but she remembered to hold Tim's hand on the roads, and she looked both ways carefully herself. Tim could feel the weight of the shoe-box in his bag, but as usual in the early morning Mr Shy was not there. Tim pondered on the problem of the seven-league boots. Maybe they would fit into his bag if he took them one at a time . . . He was still lost in thought when they arrived at school.

Some of the boys were in a huddle, discussing movies they had watched on television the night before.

'Did you watch *Dirty Harry*?' Ricky was saying. 'How about when he blasted those baddies at the end?' He danced around, making explosive sounds.

'*Jaws* was much better,' put in Ben. 'All that blood on the water when he ripped the lady apart.'

'They cut out all the best bits for television,' scoffed Colin Peters. 'I've seen it full-length on our video. It's great.'

Tim was always a little envious in these conversations, because he was never allowed to stay up and watch the eight-thirty movies. He wandered over to Phillip.

'I think violence is really boring,' said Phillip. He wasn't allowed to watch the eight-thirty movies either. 'I watched a great documentary on Channel Two, about the Yeti.'

'What's that?'

'You know – the Abominable Snowmen, in the Himalayas. These scientists claim the Yeti are definitely human – just from a different evolutionary branch. They reckon they're over two and a half metres tall.'

'Some of them are even bigger,' said Tim, recalling the two hairy figures fleeing down the mountainside. 'And the old ones get grey hair, just like people.'

'What would you know about them?'

'Oh, I saw . . . something in a book. A photo—'

'No, no, that would've been just a drawing. Artist's impression. No-one's ever photographed a Yeti. That's why some people don't believe in them. No-one's ever seen an old one with grey hair, either.'

Tim wished he'd taken his camera on his trip around the world.

After school Steffy was waiting obediently in the playground when Tim shot out of the building.

'Where've you been, Tim?'

'It wasn't fair. We had to stay in until we'd written out all the stuff on the blackboard. Two whole pages in our exercise books!'

Tim dragged Steffy along. 'Come on, if we're not home by half-past three Mum won't let us go by ourselves again.'

They hurried through the shopping centre. Tim's heart jolted as his eyes alighted on Mr Shy's shop, back in its usual place. He looked around. The bank had a clock on the wall. He pressed his face to the glass and peered in. Twenty past three. There was just time – home was only another five minutes' walk. Tim steered Steffy towards the window of the antique shop.

'I just want to see if they've got any old comics,' he explained. 'Oh, wow, Steffy. Look at that doll's house.'

Steffy was transfixed. It really was a very good doll's house – a bit faded, but crammed with funny bits of furniture, with pictures pasted on the walls and little curtains in the windows. Keeping an eye on Steffy, Tim sidestepped until he reached Mr Shy's door, then dived in.

'A young man in a hurry,' observed Mr Shy.

'Sorry, sorry, I've got to go straightaway,' panted Tim, dragging the Cinderella shoe-box out of his bag. 'They were great, thank you, but . . . I'm sorry . . . she lost one.'

'They always do,' said Mr Shy soothingly. He produced the missing slipper from under the counter and popped it into the box.

Tim gaped. 'Oh! Well . . . I've got to go. I'll bring the boots next time, if I can.' He fled, the sound of Mr Shy's wheezing following him out the door.

Steffy was watching him curiously when he rejoined her.

'Is that a shoe-shop?' she asked.

'What? Where?'

'That shop you just came out of.'

'Can you see it?' Tim was amazed.

'Not any more. It's gone.' Steffy was staring over his shoulder. Tim looked, and saw that the shop had indeed disappeared. 'It must be a magic shop,' concluded Steffy. 'Is that where you got my Cinderella shoes?'

'Look, Steffy,' said Tim earnestly. 'You've got to forget you ever saw it, OK? If you talk about it the magic will go bad, and you'll turn into a . . . a black beetle . . . or—' He struggled to think of some creature Steffy didn't like.

'A funnel-web spider?' she contributed.

'Yes. And now let's run, or we'll be late.'

They ran all the way home, and Steffy arrived so puffed out she couldn't say anything for quite a while. Their mother was watching at the gate – you could almost imagine she had been there all day, watching the street for them – and her face showed some anxiety, but she agreed that Tim had done a good job.

'You'll soon get used to it, Mum,' Tim reassured her. 'Then you won't get so worried.'

'I'll give you a week,' said his mother. 'If you get to school on time, and home on time every day, then by Friday I'll start to relax.'

The days flew past. Steffy was docile and co-operative all the time. One day she gave Tim a fright by running on ahead of him, but when she got to the road she stopped and waited for him.

'I could easily cross it by myself,' she remarked.

'I know, but Mum wouldn't like it.'

Tim was doing well at school, and Miss Barker always seemed to have a good word for him. On Wednesday they had a maths test, and he was the only person to get it all right. Miss Barker said that maybe he could think about entering a children's story-writing competition that Phillip and Kylie were going in for. The prize was a set of encyclopedias. Tim would have preferred a Lego castle, or something really terrific like that; but it would still feel good to win. Phillip was writing a complicated story about gun-running in Dar-es-Salaam. Tim found it a bit hard to follow in parts. Tim thought for a while about his own recent adventures, and decided on a story with lots of description about a tiger hunting a boy in the jungle.

Steffy went to a friend's house on Thursday after school, and Tim hoped that he would be able to have a word with Mr Shy about his difficulty in bringing back the seven-league boots. But Mr Shy was not there. He had not appeared since the previous Monday, nor had Steffy mentioned his shop again. Tim felt that the longer Mr Shy stayed out of sight, the more likely she would be to forget the whole thing. Meanwhile, Tim hurried home to start work on his story.

'Tim,' said his mother, as they sat together having afternoon tea – she had let him light the gas and pour her coffee – 'I've got a bit of a problem tomorrow.'

'Oh?' Tim looked up from his bread and honey.

'I've really got to go to the dentist – I've broken a filling, and it feels like the rest of it is loose. But the only time she can fit me in is tomorrow at a quarter to three.'

'We'll still be at school.'

'Yes, but it could take a while – or I might have to wait. I can't be sure I'll be back by three thirty. Maybe I could arrange for you to go to someone's house . . .'

'No, Mum, we'll be all right. Really. Why don't you just leave the spare key in the hiding place?'

'Well, I'm not sure . . .'

'Honestly, Mum,' Tim bounced up and down with eagerness. 'I can look after Steffy if you're late. She'll only be watching *Playschool*, and I'll have to work on my story.'

'OK, then. But you've still got to be home by three thirty, even if I'm not here.'

Later, Tim went up to his room and took out the seven-league boots. The leather was soft and supple, and he found that he could roll them up. They were still rather bulky, but it seemed to him that one could fit in his school bag. He picked up the school bag, then put it down again. He picked up one of the boots, then put it down.

The trouble was Steffy. She seemed to have forgotten all about the shoe library, and he dared not do anything to remind her. There was no telling what she might do or say. And if he tried to divert her attention and slip into the shop again, like the other day, she was sure to notice. Her sharp little eyes were everywhere.

Tim put the boots away again. Then, on second thoughts, he moved them from the dress-ups box to the back of the drawer under his bed. Steffy would never look in there.

The next day Tim got out of school early. He went down the stairs slowly, expecting a long wait in the schoolyard; but to his surprise Steffy came skipping out of her classroom, well before the bell.

'You're early too!' exclaimed Tim. 'Your teacher must be deaf.'

'Well, yours must be blind,' retorted Steffy, trotting along by his side.

They crossed the road and sauntered past the shops. It was nice, not having to hurry, for a change. The bookshop had a competition going. You had to guess how many sweets were in the huge glass jar displayed in the window. If you were right, you got the jar, and also a twenty-dollar book voucher. That would be enough for that great pop-up book, the one about the haunted house.

'Let's go in for it!' said Steffy. 'I bet the answer's a million.'

'It costs fifty cents to enter,' Tim pointed out. 'Maybe Mum will give us the money on Monday. I reckon I can work out how many there are . . .'

He pressed his nose to the glass, counting intently. There were about fifty-three layers, if you counted a line of sweets from the bottom to the top . . . fifteen sweets across that you could see, so maybe another fifteen that you couldn't see, just around the outside, or would it be more? Gosh, he'd have to borrow Mum's calculator! Plus the ones at the top where the jar got thinner . . .

Tim straightened up and looked around. Steffy had gone. She must have wandered on along the street. He scanned the footpath. There weren't many people around at this time of day, so he could see a long way. No Steffy. He looked back the way they had come. No-one.

Maybe she was in the newsagent's. She was always at him to go in there and look at the toys they kept down the back. Tim retraced his steps and went in. He had to go right through the shop to look properly, but she was not there.

Tim hurried outside and along the street. An unpleasant thought was forming inside him, and he realized what it was when he reached the hairdresser's. Mr Shy's shop was there. Tim rushed in.

132

The shop was cool and dim, as usual. It took Tim's eyes a few moments to get used to the darkness. Mr Shy was not to be seen.

'Mr Shy?' Tim called softly, peering towards the gloom at the far end of the shop. He reached for the silver bell, but as his fingers touched it the top half of Mr Shy appeared. He had evidently been bending down, doing something under the counter, and now he stood, gazing gravely at Tim.

'Is my little sister here?' demanded Tim.

Mr Shy clasped his hands on the counter and looked at them. There was a strange expression on his face. If Tim hadn't known him better, he would have said that Mr Shy was worried.

'You understand,' began Mr Shy at last, 'that as Librarian I can give a certain amount of . . . guidance . . . but beyond merely advising I am not . . . permitted . . . insofar as my job description . . .'

'All I want to know,' interrupted Tim impatiently, 'is whether my sister Steffy is here.'

'Ah . . . no.'

'But she was here.' Tim suddenly understood Mr Shy's strange mood. 'That's it, isn't it? And you gave her some shoes?'

'She is entitled to borrow. I can only . . . make certain recommendations . . .'

'What did she get? Was it something awful?' All sorts of dreadful visions flashed through Tim's mind. 'Oh, Mr Shy – it wasn't those red shoes, was it?'

'I can advise against . . . but I am not permitted to say what consequences . . . She insisted on the red shoes.'

Tim still couldn't remember the story, but he knew it had given him nightmares. Something about a girl who had to dance until she died . . .

'I suppose you could consider going after her,' said Mr Shy, looking very guilty.

'How can I find her?'

'Walk backwards in the seven-league boots, one step at a time,' said Mr Shy.

'Can't you give me any more help than that? What will happen to her? You must know—'

Mr Shy leaned over the counter. 'Think twice about following her, boy,' he urged. 'You'll have to go through the Four Elements.'

Tim was fed up with Mr Shy's mysterious advice. 'Just tell me where to start looking,' he insisted.

Mr Shy shrugged. 'Does she have a red ballet dress?'

Tim was out the door before Mr Shy had finished, and tearing along the street. His rasping breath beat out a faster rhythm than his feet as they thudded on the pavement. 'Please, Steffy,' he prayed. 'Walk slowly, or forget where the spare key is hidden, or have a long search for your dress.'

But lying like a heavy weight on his chest was the conviction that he was going to be too late.

Chapter 13

The back door was ajar when Tim reached it, the spare key in the lock.

'Steffy?'

He bounded up the stairs two at a time. At the door of their room he nearly tripped over Steffy's school bag. Her school clothes were strewn across the floor. The kitten was sitting up on Steffy's bed with that sleepy, ruffled look he always got when woken up suddenly. Tim looked into the dress-ups box, knowing what he would see. The red ballet dress Steffy had got for her birthday had gone.

'Steffy! Steffy!' Tim called. The room remained silent and still. The kitten yawned and stretched.

Tim dived for the drawer under his bed. The kitten jumped on to the bed and peered into the drawer with him. The seven-league boots were still there. Tim dragged them on and stood up.

'Here goes,' he said, taking a deep breath and a big step backwards.

'What now?' said Tim. He was in a sort of forest. It was dim and gloomy and deep-green and damp, with a decaying, rotten smell, and every surface covered with layer upon layer of moss. The raucous cries of many birds and animals filled the air, but they were almost drowned out themselves by the sound of rushing water. Tim shivered, partly remembering the tiger which had stalked him, but partly because this forest, unlike the jungle, was cold.

Tim started to run. His seven-league boots did not send him off in huge strides in this place, so he was able to run normally. He ran towards the light and the sound of water. The forest was so dense there was really no other direction in which he could go. Before long he found himself on the bank of a roaring, fast-flowing river. It looked deep and dark, and there was no way across. He looked around. Upstream the river emerged from a dark, steep-sided gorge, and the bank was narrow and slippery. Downstream the bank was wider and flatter. Tim decided to go that way.

On Tim's side of the river the forest was very close to the water, and cast sombre shadows; but on the opposite bank he could see a big, grassy meadow, dotted with flowers. Straining his eyes, he thought he could see something moving. Far away on the other side of the river, a flash of red flickered against the green grass. She was dancing like a mad thing, skipping and leaping across the meadow.

'Steffy!' called Tim. 'Steffy!'

She caught sight of him and waved. 'Look at me, Tim!' Her voice was carried faintly across the water. 'Look at me dance!'

'Steffy, wait! I'm coming over!'

'Can't stop!' Steffy called gaily, dancing on to a little track that led away from the meadow into some long grass beyond.

'No, Steffy! Wait!' Tim darted down the river bank to where some rocks lay strewn in the water as though thrown there by some bad-tempered giant. Up close, the rocks were wet and dark with moss. There were big ones and little ones, and they did seem close enough together to use as stepping stones. The water surged around them, throwing up showers of spray.

Tim stepped on to the first rock and teetered there dangerously. After a moment he felt he had his balance, so he stepped cautiously on to another rock.

Halfway across the rocks seemed further apart. He had to make a little run and jump on to a big rock. He landed well enough, but the rock was covered in a brownish moss which was very slippery, and Tim found himself sliding off it. He landed in water up to his knees, but he could feel his feet slipping on more rocks below the surface, and the current was pulling at his legs. Groping around wildly, he grabbed a big branch which looked as though it might form a bridge to the next rock; but as Tim clambered on to it the branch became dislodged, and the current caught it and swept it away down the river.

Tim scrambled into a sitting position on the branch. It was moving rapidly down the river, and there was nothing he could do to stop it. The water was flowing even faster than Tim had thought, and here and there it was slapping against sharp rocks that stuck up, hurling white spray into the air. It seemed to Tim that the river was getting narrower, and that the rocks were more and more frequent. Then, above the surging sound of the water around him, he heard another louder, duller, deeper roar.

Tim grabbed the branch, which was now pitching and tossing wildly in the rough water. Ahead, the river disappeared. Simply disappeared into blue sky and billows of fine white spray. They were racing towards that dreadful nothingness. Tim looked around despairingly. He was not far from the river's edge, and a few dead trees stood in the shallows, their branches overhanging the water. Perhaps he could grab one . . . With great difficulty he got to his feet, balancing on the slippery branch like someone on a surf-board. He wished he hadn't been too scared to take up his cousin Jason's offer to teach him surfing last summer holidays. He reached for a tree – and missed by a mile. And there, right in front of him, where he could not fail to crash into it, was a needle-sharp rock. Instinctively, Tim jumped backwards.

Tim sat up and looked around. He was lying on a rough, stony slope. He seemed to be on a high mountainside, but it was warm, even hot. Steam was rising from his wet clothes. There was neither sight nor sound of the river.

'I stepped backwards in the seven-league boots!' he said, as realization dawned. 'I wish I'd thought of that sooner.'

He stood up and looked around, trying to work out which way to go. There was a sort of hot wind blowing, and a strange smell in the air. Away to his left he could see another slope, covered with

pine trees. He wondered if it was part of the forest near the river, but it looked too high. Not far to his left was a pile of huge boulders, and he picked his way across to them, intending to climb up for a better look.

Suddenly there was a deafening roar which seemed to fill the air. The ground shook, and the sky went black. Dense clouds of smoke and ash swirled around Tim, making him cough and choke. Looking back to where he had been standing, he saw that the spot had been engulfed in a stream of liquid fire, which was surging and bubbling down the slope, and spreading towards him. Tim scrambled up the pile of boulders as the lava swirled around his feet. Some of the smaller rocks at ground level were picked up and swept down the hill, but the larger ones seemed heavy enough to stay in place.

Tim climbed as high as he could, teetering on the top of what had become an island. He could now see that beyond his pile of boulders the same thing was happening, except that the ground was more uneven, and the lava stream had broken up into small rivulets, which were pouring down the mountainside, separating and joining up at random. From here, too, he could see the top of the mountain, which was belching steam, thick smoke and great hiccups of fiery red spray.

The heat on his face made Tim turn away, but something made him look back at the rough ground and there, a deeper red against the fiery rivers, was Steffy. She was dancing wildly in the narrowing gaps between the lava, jumping over smaller streams, leaping from one sharp rock to another.

'No, Steffy, no!' he screamed. 'Get away from there!'

The swirling wind must have carried his voice, because she looked up and saw him. She waved

gaily and seemed about to dance towards him, but then she spun around and went leaping off in the opposite direction. Soon he lost sight of her in the clouds of smoke.

'Steffy!' sobbed Tim. 'Where are you?'

He clambered about on his pile of rocks. There was no way down – he was surrounded by bubbling, hissing lava, which was rising every second as more and more came pouring down the mountain.

There was only one choice: he had to trust the boots and step backwards again. He could feel the unbearable heat of the lava, and he could imagine what it would be like to fall into it.

Tim screwed his eyes tightly shut, held his breath and took a big step backwards.

He landed with a jarring thud, and opened his eyes. Or did he? Everything was pitch black. Tim rubbed his eyes. They were open. He groped around in mounting terror. Was he inside the crater of the volcano? But no, it was cool here, and the burning, acrid smell was gone. Feeling about, his fingers found something hard – yet crumbly – a sort of wall. It was cold and slightly damp. He listened. There was silence, except for a steady drip, drip, drip, somewhere nearby.

But Tim's eyes were getting used to the darkness, and he found that there was some faint light getting in from somewhere – enough for him to see that he was in a sort of tunnel, with earth sides and a damp, earthy floor.

He groped his way along one wall, and found that it soon led to a sort of intersection, with three or four other tunnels going off in different directions. One of them seemed to be sloping upwards a little, so he began to follow that, only to find it dropping steeply again. He stopped and listened. The dripping sound was fainter now, but there was something else – a sort of scuffling, pattering noise. Maybe it was rats. Tim shivered at the thought. But there was something rhythmical about the sound . . .

'Steffy?' he called tentatively.

'Tim!' Her voice was startlingly close. 'Where are you?'

'I . . . I don't know. Above you, I think. Try to come towards the sound of my voice.'

'What?' Her voice was fainter now. 'I can't hear you.'

'This way, Steffy,' called Tim desperately. 'Turn around. Keep going upwards.'

'My feet hurt, Tim.' Her plaintive voice was closer to him. 'And it's dark. I want to stop dancing now.'

'Take the shoes off, Steffy!' Surely her voice had come from down this tunnel, maybe a little to the left. Tim groped his way towards it.

'I can't!' Her voice was fainter again, fading away. 'I can't stop . . .'

Tim found the tunnel branching into three. Which way? 'You must, Steffy!' he shouted. 'Take the shoes off. Try!'

He seemed to have come out into a cave, and his voice echoed mockingly around the walls. 'Try! Try! Try!'

When the echoes had died away, Tim listened.

Silence. 'Steffy!' he called. 'Steffy! Steffy! Steffy!'
jeered the echoes. Tim darted down the nearest
tunnel, tripping over clods of earth in the dark.
After another few metres he ran straight into
another earth wall, grazing his forehead. It was a
dead end.

Tim slumped to his knees. His forehead was

stinging, and he felt blood trickling down his face. The pain, slight though it was, seemed to release something locked up deep inside him, and he buried his face in his hands and cried in great racking sobs. He would never find Steffy now. He would have to take the boots off and go home without her, and somehow tell his mother and his father that she was gone forever, and that it was all his fault. Or if he couldn't face doing that, he would have to stay in this dismal place until he died.

He stood up and took a few deep breaths. His father always said you should do that when you needed to calm down. There was one other way after all. He would use the seven-league boots to go on searching until he found Steffy, and he would bring her back. He wiped his eyes with a clean bit of his T-shirt, then took a big step backwards.

Nothing happened.

Tim reached down and felt the boots. They were on properly. He tried another step backwards. Still nothing happened. He took a step forward. Nothing unusual. Either the magic had worn off the boots, or he was so far underground that not even magic worked.

Now, thought Tim, I've really got something to cry about. But his tears were all used up, and instead his mind was racing. There must be a way out. Air was getting in from somewhere, and light too. If he could find another tunnel that sloped upwards . . . Maybe that was what Steffy had done. Tim refused to think about the possibility that she had gone further into the labyrinth.

Starting at the big open cave, he began method-ically to explore. Every few metres a new tunnel opened off the cave. Some were dead ends, like the first one he had tried. Some went steeply down-wards. Some started level, or even sloping up, but ultimately went on the same downward course as the others. At last his efforts were rewarded with a tunnel that started fairly level, then gradually sloped upwards. Tim followed it cautiously, not daring to believe his luck. A couple of times it branched into two, but he always seemed to have found the right branch to follow. Finally he felt sure it was getting lighter and then, rounding a bend, he was almost blinded by a rush of daylight spilling in through a hole in the roof. He clambered upwards, tearing his fingernails on the rough rocks, and emerged in pale sunshine.

Tim lay gasping on the ground for a few moments, exhausted by his efforts. Then he sat up and looked around. He was on another mountain-side, but this mountain was steeper and more jagged than the last. It had a narrow path winding upwards – downwards, too, of course, except that a fall of rocks had completely blocked it just below the spot where Tim had emerged.

Far away, beyond several other dizzying moun-tain peaks, Tim could see the volcano still in pro-gress, spurting great fountains of fire high into the air; and far below him, through breaks in the swirling mist, was the brown river curling down the valley, and the dark forest beyond. The only sound was the thin whistling of the wind. It was cold. Tim would have expected to see snow on mountains this high, but there was none. The path, however, was slippery with ice, and Tim eyed it with some alarm. There was no other way to go, however, so he stepped out cautiously.

Upward climbed Tim. The air was colder and thinner, and the wind howled dismally. The narrow path was flanked by a sheer rock face on one side, a terrible drop into the mist on the other; and it must have wound several times right around the mountain on its steep upward journey.

Sometimes when Tim rounded a bend the full force of the wind would hit him, forcing him to flatten himself against the rock face and creep along sideways, for fear of being blown over the edge.

Every now and then he stopped and called 'Steffy!' and sometimes in the answering wail of the wind he thought he heard a faint 'Tim!'. At last he came to a place where he could see ahead to where the mountain disappeared into thick cloud and there, high above him, he saw a familiar red-clad figure flitting along on the cliff edge.

'Wait for me!' he yelled, breaking into a run.

Steffy was drooping, her face tear-stained. Sometimes she seemed about to sink to her knees, but then her feet would take control again and her whole body would convulse into a frenzied dance. 'I want to stop, Tim!' she called.

'Turn around, Steffy. Come down to me. I'll help you!'

'I can't!' she cried. 'My feet want to go up there.'

146

'Dance on the spot, then. Let me get to you!'
Tim was scrambling desperately towards her. In
places the path was so steep he had to go on hands
and knees. Once, in a section where he was able to
run, his foot slipped near the edge, sending showers
of stones cascading into space.

At last the path began to flatten out. He rounded
a bend, and found himself on a small level area,
hardly as big as a room. The mountain dropped
away on all sides. The path up which Tim had
come was the only way up or down.

Steffy was spinning and leaping in circles, but
as he approached her feet seemed to fly into a
panic and she danced away from him, towards the
edge. Her feet drummed wildly on the path, looking for an escape.

'Help me, Tim!' Her head was turned towards
him, but her madly dancing feet were dragging her
away, towards the cliff-edge.

'No!' screamed Tim. Everything seemed to
happen in slow motion. Steffy danced on to the
edge of the cliff and leapt out into space. At the
same time Tim dived. His hands closed around
Steffy's feet . . . and he found himself lying face-
down, his head and shoulders dangling over the
edge of the cliff, the red shoes in his hands. He
looked down, down into the swirling mist. There
was no sign of Steffy, no sound except the wailing
wind.

Tim sat up. He was shivering uncontrollably.
He looked with hatred at the shoes in his hands,
then he stood up and threw them as high and as
far as he could over the edge. They flashed bright

147

red in the faint sunlight, then they were gone. In a
frenzy of despair Tim dragged off one of his boots
and hurled it over the edge, too. He tugged at the
other boot . . .

Chapter 14

Tim's head was aching. He stirred uneasily in his bed and opened one eye. The room was very light. Had he slept in again? Somewhere he could hear his mother calling. "Tim? Tim, are you up there?'

Memory came flooding back as he sat up and looked around. He was lying on top of the blanket, still in his clothes – very dirty, and his T-shirt was ripped – but with nothing on his feet. He was alone in the room.

'Tim? Where are you?'

'Coming.'

With a heavy heart he got to his feet. Now he would have to tell his mother the whole story. Of course she wouldn't believe him. She'd call the police, and they'd search and search for Steffy, but they'd never find her. Tim felt a terrible lump in his throat. He must keep the tears back until he had spoken.

He walked slowly down the stairs and into the living-room. His mother turned a horror-struck face towards him.

'Tim! What have you done?'

'I'm sorry, Mum . . .' Despite his efforts his nose was starting to run and his eyelids prickled. 'I tried to look after her . . .'

But suddenly a whirlwind from the kitchen engulfed him, nearly knocking his over.

'Tim! Tim!' It was Steffy, still in her red ballet dress, a piece of bread dripping honey in one hand while she hugged him with the other. 'I thought you'd never come back!'

'What is going on here?' asked their mother in her sternest voice, but at the same time she scooped Tim on to her knee and held him while he shook with sobs, unable to speak. 'I come home to find no-one here, though you'd both obviously been here, and I go searching the streets. Then Steffy turns up with her feet cut to shreds, trailing blood everywhere, and Tim appears to have been upstairs all the time – or where *have* you been, Tim? And what have you done to your forehead?'

'It's all my fault,' began Steffy quickly. 'We came straight home – we were early, weren't we Tim? And I wanted to show my red ballet dress to . . . to Cassandra, so I put it on and I sneaked out, and I didn't tell Tim because I knew he wouldn't let me go, and I didn't even wear any shoes, but of course there was broken glass . . .'

'And you went off searching for her?' their mother gently asked Tim.

'Yes,' he managed. 'And I couldn't find her, and I hit my head on the wall, and I thought she was dead . . . and now you'll never let me look after her again . . .' He buried his face in his mother's shoulder and let the tears flow.

'Oh, dear. Come on, Tim, darling. Pull yourself together.' She cuddled him closer, patting him soothingly. Steffy crept up on the other side.

'I'm sorry, Tim,' she murmured. 'I won't run away from you ever again.'

The kitten jumped on to their mother's knee too, and nestled in. Finally she managed to untangle them all and lead Tim to the bathroom. His face in the mirror was almost unrecognizable; smeared with blood, and with long streaks where the tears had streamed through the dirt. No wonder she had been so horrified at the sight of him.

'I'll have to think about this,' she said, gently washing his face, while Steffy sat nearby, bathing her feet in a basin, 'but it looks to me as if you did the right thing, Tim. If Steffy was naughty enough to disappear like that, I don't really see how you could have stopped her. If she'll promise to be good, I think you can go on bringing her home from school.'

Later, when he and Steffy were alone, Tim said, 'But how did you get back here? I was sure you'd gone over the cliff.'

'I don't know,' she said. 'I just felt something grab at the shoes, and I felt them come off – and there I was, lying on the grass outside, and kitty was sitting on top of me, purring.'

'How did you get on to that mountain, anyway?' asked Tim.

'I did it by spinning around.'

'How do you mean?'

'Well, every time I did a kind of twirly thing, in my dance, I'd suddenly be somewhere else – like those burning rivers, and those spooky tunnels.' Steffy shuddered. 'Tim, I don't want any more magic shoes.'

152

'Neither do I, Steffy. Not for a long, long time.'

All the next week, going to school and back, they kept their eyes open for Mr Shy. They should at least go into the shop, and explain to him how they had lost two pairs of shoes in one go. Tim hoped there wouldn't be a fine, even though Steffy had offered to pay it out of her birthday money.

But Mr Shy's shop did not appear. The part of the street where it had been seemed to look more ordinary than ever – it was harder each day to imagine Mr Shy suddenly appearing there.

'I don't think he's coming back,' said Steffy at last. 'He probably thinks we're dead.'

Tim felt a shiver run down his back. Sometimes in his dreams he saw Steffy again, plunging over the cliff. In the dreams he dived for the shoes, and his hands closed over empty air.

'Mum, what are the Four Elements?' he asked one day.

'Four elements? Oh well, there's hydrogen, oxygen, carbon, iron, potassium . . . Why do you want to know?'

'Not four elements, Mum. *The* Four Elements.'

'Well . . .' she thought for a moment. 'Could mean the weather . . . Is this something you've seen in a book?'

'Sort of.'

'There's one thing . . . In the old days, before people understood about – you know – atoms, they thought everything was made up of four sorts of matter. They called them the four elements. There was air, earth, fire and water.'

'Water, fire, earth and air?'

'Yes, that's right.'

Tim was very quiet for a while, remembering the raging river, the roaring volcano, the dank underground tunnels and Steffy plunging into space on the windswept mountain-top.

By the end of the week Tim and Steffy had stopped wondering about Mr Shy, with the excitement of their father coming home. They were picked up from school early on Friday, so they could be at the airport on time. Then there was what seemed like hours of waiting around. Tim and Steffy went out on to the windy observation deck, and there was much excitement when a speck appeared in the sky, rapidly growing into a big Qantas jumbo jet which swooped past them and landed, turning to taxi slowly towards the terminal.

'I can see him! I can see him!' shrieked Steffy.

'You can't.'

'I can! I can see his arm waving to us!'

They ran to find their mother.

'It's landed!' cried Steffy. 'A big Qantas one. I saw Daddy!'

'He's flying American this time,' said her mother gently. 'But he has landed, over on the other side of the terminal.'

Then there was another interminable wait outside the customs area, as baggage-laden passengers trickled out; and suddenly there he was, bigger and louder than anyone remembered, hugging them all at once, and Tim and Steffy were talking at the tops of their voices, and Mum was laughing and wiping her eyes.

Then there were presents to be distributed, including a magic set for Tim. Not real magic, of course, but some very neat tricks, with a book explaining how to do them. Mum bustled around preparing the celebration dinner, and Steffy insisted on setting the table with all the best plates and the silver cutlery. Tim wandered upstairs to see if his father wanted help unpacking.

'How's my boy?' said his father, giving him another hug. 'You've grown up since I've been away.'

'I sure have, Dad.' What if he told Dad now about Mr Shy? Dad might think he was being babyish, like years ago when he had an imaginary friend.

'I can climb the tree in the park, near school,' Tim said.

'Good on you.'

Tim watched as his father unpacked neatly folded shirts. He was always so well-organized.

'Are you staying home for a long time, Dad?'

'Well, I thought I was, son – but that's something I wanted to talk to you about.'

Tim's heart sank. He knew what was coming: another urgent call, another long trip. 'I know. Where are you going this time?'

'Looks like they need me in Denmark. That's one place I've never been, Tim. It's a big job, too – six months, they reckon.'

Tim stared at his father in dismay. 'Denmark? For six months?'

'Six months,' said his father. 'So I put my foot

down. I'll go, I said – but only if my family comes too. Your mother likes the idea.'

'All of us?' Tim was stunned.

'You, Mum and Steffy. The question is, do you want to go?'

'Oh, boy!' The implications dawned on Tim. 'Denmark! They have lots of ice and snow there. Denmark! That's where Legoland is! Oh boy! Do I want to go! Does Steffy know?' He rushed to the door, then turned back. 'What about kitty, Dad?'

'I'm sure Auntie Marjorie will have him for a while. It'll be a holiday for him.'

'Right. That's good,' said Tim. 'He needs a holiday. Can I tell Steffy, Dad? I can't wait to see her face.'

'We'll both tell her,' smiled his father. 'I want to see her face too.' He closed the last drawer, threw an arm around Tim's shoulder, and they walked down the stairs together.

THE END

TIME OUT

BY HELEN CRESSWELL

'All you've got to do,' said Wilkes, 'is say one
spell and the next thing you know, you're
there.'

Tweeny can hardly believe her ears. First (to
the horror of Cook), the cat turns green and
then her father, the butler in a very respectable
Victorian household, announces that he can do
magic spells! Even more exciting, now he's
suggesting that the whole family use The Hundred Year Spell to travel forward a hundred
years for their holidays . . .

SBN 0 440 862086

YEARLING BOOKS

CHIMNEY WITCH CHASE

BY VICTORIA WHITEHEAD

'Who's for some roof races, goblins?' Rufus cried. The idea went down a treat and the goblins stopped throwing things about and danced in a circle, jumping on and off the furniture.

From a mad rooftop party to a wild broomstick ride, an enchanted wood and a disorderly gang of goblins, Ellen's friendship with Rufus, the mischievous witch boy living in her chimney, leads her into one hilarious adventure after another.

SBN 0 440 86206X

YEARLING BOOKS

A DRAGON IN SPRING-TERM

BY JUNE COUNSEL

'Here we are,' cried Scales cheerfully. 'Spring on Magic Mountain!'

Sam and his friends in Class 4 have a very special friend – a young dragon called Scales. They are all looking forward to seeing him when they go back to school for the Spring term. But Miss Green, their teacher, has put his cage away in the stockroom and firmly tells them that this term they will be doing new things, starting with a computer . . .

However, all dragons wake up in the spring, and soon Scales is back with Sam and his friends, leading them all up to Magic Mountain for a series of wonderful adventures!

An amusing and lively fantasy for young readers.

SBN 0 440 862094

YEARLING BOOKS

If you would like to receive a Newsletter about our new Children's books, just fill in the coupon below with your name and address (or copy it onto a separate piece of paper if you don't want to spoil your book) and send it to:

The Children's Books Editor
Transworld Publishers Ltd.
61–63 Uxbridge Road,
Ealing
London W5 5SA

Please send me a Children's Newsletter:

Name . . . .

Address . . . .

. . . .

. . . .

All Children's Books are available at your bookshop or newsagent, or can be ordered from the following address:
Transworld Publishers Ltd.,
Cash Sales Department,
P.O. Box 11, Falmouth, Cornwall TR10 9EN

Please send a cheque or postal order (no currency) and allow 80p for postage and packing for the first book plus 20p for each additional book ordered up to a maximum charge of £2.00 in UK.

B.F.P.O. customers please allow 80p for the first book and 20p for each additional book.

Overseas customers, including Eire, please allow £1.50 for postage and packing for the first book, £1.00 for the second book, and 30p for each subsequent title ordered.